BEST-LOVED
FAIRY TALES

BEST-LOVED
FAIRY TALES

Retold and introduced by Neil Philip

Illustrated by Isabelle Brent

A LITTLE, BROWN BOOK

First published by Little, Brown in 2007

Text copyright © 2007 Neil Philip
Illustrations copyright © 2007 Isabelle Brent

ISBN 978-0-316-02755-7

Designed by Tegan Sharrard
Produced by Omnipress, UK
Printed and bound in Singapore

Little, Brown
An imprint of
Little Brown Book Group
Brettenham House
Lancaster Place
London WC2E 7EN

www.littlebrown.co.uk

A member of the Hachette Livre Group of Companies

For
Olive and Louis James
N.P.

For
Robert D. Symonds
I.B.

Contents

 # The Fairy Tales

Fairy tales by The Brothers Grimm and Hans Christian Andersen.

About the Authors

Hans Christian Andersen

Andersen was born in Denmark in 1805. He wrote over a hundred and fifty fairy tales, as well as plays, poems, novels and lively accounts of his travels. When he died in 1875 he was one of the most famous writers in the world, and his fairy tales remain as popular as ever.

The Brothers Grimm

Jacob and Wilhelm Grimm were born in 1785 and 1786, and died in 1863 and 1859, respectively. The brothers remained very close all through their lives, sharing a house even after Wilhelm's marriage to Dortchen Wild, from whom the brothers recorded several fairy tales. Although their fame depends on their collection of German fairy tales, they were also notable scholars of German literature and language. They are regarded as the founding fathers of folktale research.

HANS CHRISTIAN ANDERSEN

INTRODUCTION

O N Sunday, September 18, 1825, the young Hans Christian Andersen
– still a struggling and rather immature schoolboy at the age of
twenty – confided to his diary: "I must carry out my work! I must
paint for mankind the vision that stands before my soul in all its vividness
and diversity; my soul knows that it can and will do this."

Though he was from a poor family and knew no one, this earnest young
man had been taken up by some of Denmark's most influential people; the
king himself approved a grant from a royal fund to provide his belated
education, and future grants were to support the struggling writer.

Andersen's curious combination of hypersensitivity and unshakeable self-
belief nakedly displayed in *The Diaries of Hans Christian Andersen* (1990)
– carried him through numerous false starts until he found the medium in
which he could paint his vision for mankind: the fairy tale. In Andersen's
hands this art form – the storytelling vehicle of the dreams and longings of
the unlettered – became a subtle method of autobiography. Andersen himself
takes the central role in nearly all his tales, whether disguised as a student, a
gardener, a mermaid or a shirt collar; when he came to publish an actual
autobiography, he entitled it *The Fairy Tale of My Life*.

In that book, Andersen recalls how as a child he often used to visit the
spinning-room of the pauper hospital and asylum in Odense, Denmark, where

he was brought up. The old women there, entertained by Andersen's childish prattle, rewarded him "by telling me tales in return; and thus a world as rich as that of *The Thousand and One Nights* was revealed to me". That rich world of the Danish folk tale – later harvested by collectors such as Evald Tang Kristensen, and analysed by folklorist Bengt Holbek in his book *The Interpretation of Fairy Tales* (1987) – formed the soil in which Andersen's creativity could flower.

In 1857, Andersen stayed with Charles Dickens in England for five weeks. Although the two men had great respect for each other, the visit was a strain – Dickens's daughter Kate cruelly but succinctly summed up the family's view when she recalled, "He was a bony bore, and stayed on and on." Dickens himself – scrupulously polite and attentive to his guest – relieved his feelings afterwards by sticking a notice on the dressing-room mirror which read, "Hans Andersen slept in this room for five weeks – which seemed to the family AGES!"

The main problem was that Andersen's spoken English was almost incomprehensible. Andersen's first translator, Mary Howitt, spitefully assured Dickens that in fact Andersen didn't know Danish either. There is an edge to this comment. Andersen's Danish is not the severe, highflown literary Danish of his day – it is raw and unpolished, and in it one is always aware of the speaking voice. This directness and informality, both of phrasing and rhythm, stem directly from the storytelling of the old women in the Odense spinning-room, and they are one of the reasons why Andersen's fairy tales have stayed so fresh and appealing.

This colloquial quality was not always apparent in Victorian translations such as Mary Howitt's, which gave Andersen's tales a genteel and overworked air; one of my aims in making these new versions of some of Andersen's finest tales is to follow modern translators such as R. P. Keigwin and Brian Alderson in capturing his relaxed and intimate storytelling voice.

Interestingly, Andersen *did* connect with the Dickens children, when he was able to tell them stories, not with his voice, but with his scissors. Henry Dickens recalled, "He had one beautiful accomplishment, which was the cutting out in paper, with an ordinary pair of scissors, of lovely little figures of sprites and elves, gnomes, fairies and animals of all kinds, which might well have stepped out of the pages of his books. These figures turned out to be quite delightful in their refinement and delicacy in design and touch."

Many of Andersen's paper cuttings survive: they can be seen at the H. C. Andersen Museum in Odense, or enjoyed in books such as Beth Wagner Brust's *The Amazing Paper Cuttings of Hans Christian Andersen* (1994). In "Little Ida's Flowers," Andersen portrays himself as the student who entertains Ida with both stories and paper cuttings; the cuttings themselves play a key role in "The Steadfast Tin Soldier."

Stories such as "Little Ida's Flowers" and "The Little Match Girl", which have always been among his most popular, have led some modern writers – for instance John Goldthwaite in *The Natural History of Make-Believe* (1996) – to criticize Andersen for his "sentimentality". Yet this "sentimentality" of Andersen's is a strange thing. At the heart of his vision of the world lies the ability to find comedy in tragedy. Story after story ends sadly in rejection, humiliation, or disappointment, yet they are saved from self-pity by the "salt" of Andersen's wit and by the acuteness of his observation.

That Andersen is essentially a poet of human suffering can be seen in one of his finest and most famous stories, "The Little Mermaid." Andersen felt driven to write this original fairy tale, of which he wrote that while "only an adult can understand its deeper meaning" nevertheless "I believe a child will enjoy it for the story's sake." The story is now perhaps best known in Disney's more optimistic version – but the deeper meaning resides in

Andersen's bleak and painful original.

"The Little Mermaid" was the first fairy tale in which Andersen attempted to explore his spiritual beliefs. A later story, "The Bell", expresses his deep faith in the beauty and holiness of the world, and the promise of new life and redemption beyond it. In it, two boys, one "a king's son", the other a pauper, make their way by separate routes – one in sunshine, the other in shadow – to the same transcendent moment at the end of their (life's) journey.

Both of the boys in this strange and moving tale are depictions of Andersen himself – they reassure him, and us, that a humble beginning and a difficult path will not make any difference in the end. The story, published in 1842, looks back to 1819, Andersen's confirmation year – the year in which he met and played with a real king's son, Prince Frederik, the future King Frederik VII of Denmark. In later life Andersen and Frederik were on close terms; Elias Bredsdorff records in *Hans Christian Andersen: The Story of His Life and Work* (1975) that the king treated the storyteller "almost like an old friend".

In 1987, the Danish historian Jens Jørgensen published an extraordinary and controversial book entitled *H. C. Andersen: En Sand Myte* (*H. C. Andersen: A True Myth*), in which he constructed an intricate web of circumstantial evidence to support his theory that Andersen was in fact the illegitimate son of King Christian VIII (Prince Frederik's father) and Countess Elise Ahlefeldt-Laurvig.

Jørgensen makes a good case both that such a child existed, and that Andersen himself was quite possibly "adopted" by his impoverished parents. He also establishes a pattern of royal and aristocratic patronage of the gawky pauper boy which suggests that someone important was keeping a weather eye out for the lad.

Though he does not firmly establish his theory as fact, Jørgensen does show that Andersen himself probably came to believe it. In a diary entry for January 3, 1875, the last year of his life, Andersen remarks how many letters he has received, then adds drily, "One has my name and address: King Christian the Ninth."

This intriguing theory, which caused a sensation in Denmark, has been rejected by some scholars, such as Elias Bredsdorff. But while it must be treated with caution, it does provide a fascinating new context in which to view the "fairy tale" of Andersen's life, and in which to read a story such as "The Bell". Is it of significance that the boy is always described as "a king's son", never as "a prince"? Was Andersen imagining how much easier his life's path might have been, if his childish boastings that he was really "a changed child of noble birth" were true? If so, his conclusion is that the path in sunshine and the path in shadow lead to the same final destination.

It was about "The Bell" that Andersen made his famous comment that his fairy tales "lay in my mind like seed-corn, requiring only a mountain stream, a ray of sunshine, a drop of wormwood, for them to spring forth and burst into bloom".

Nearly two hundred years after his birth, his garden of fairy tales is still in full flower.

NEIL PHILIP

THE BROTHERS
GRIMM

INTRODUCTION

The collection of German fairy tales made at the beginning of the nineteenth century by the brothers Jacob and Wilhelm Grimm was the first work of its kind, and it remains the most famous. It has only one rival – the fairy tales of the Danish writer Hans Christian Andersen. But there is an essential difference between the two. Andersen made up his stories; the Grimms collected theirs from folk tradition.

This divide between Andersen's creative approach and the Grimms' scholarly one led to embarassment when Andersen called on the brothers unannounced in the summer of 1844. Though Andersen was already famous, Jacob had no idea who he was, and had never even heard his name. The Grimms later made friends with Andersen, and realized that they had even printed one of his stories, "The Princess and the Pea", in their 1843 edition, thinking it a genuine folktale.

The Grimms had published the first edition of their *Kinder- und Hausmärchen* (*Children's and Household Tales*) in 1812, and continued revising and enlarging it until the seventh edition of 1857, which is the basis of most modern translations, and of my own free but faithful retellings. Their original aim was to record the folktales of Germany with unvarnished accuracy. This was a new and revolutionary idea, and it remains the foundation stone of all folktale research.

Some recent writers (such as John M. Ellis in his combative work *One Fairy Story Too Many: The Brothers Grimm and Their Tales*, 1983) have taken them to task for not carrying out this work with the strictness modern scholarship requires. They did not often identify their sources; they destroyed their manuscripts; they blended two or more tellings into single tales; and worst of all they continually tinkered with the language and even the plots of the tales to achieve maximum impact.

These criticisms are valid, but, as the essays in James M. McGlathery's excellent *The Brothers Grimm and Folktale* (1988) show, they have been taken too far. The Grimms had no model for their work; they had to invent the science of folklore as they went along. The final result may not be a word-for-word transcription of oral storytelling in a community, but it is nevertheless an authentic collection of genuine folk stories.

Wilhelm Grimm – who was responsible for most of the writing and revision – was searching for a way to voice and shape traditional oral tales on the printed page. His lively versions triumphantly convey the directness and immediacy of oral storytelling, fixing the stories in a form that catches their essence and still speaks to us today.

Whatever its status as scholarship, the Grimms' collection of fairy tales is certainly a classic of children's literature. This new selection of stories contains some of their best-known tales, such as "The Frog Prince", "Rumpelstiltskin", and "Snow White", as well as some of their short comic stories, chosen to counter the widespread impression that all their tales are Grimm by name and grim by nature. There is cruelty and darkness in Grimm, but there is comedy and light as well.

The Grimms themselves were lifelong collaborators. Jacob, the more scholarly of the two, was born in 1785 and died in 1863. Wilhelm, the more literary, was born in 1786 and died in 1859. Their pioneering collections of

German fairy tales and legends are not their only monument: they also initiated the great German dictionary, *Deutsches Wörterbuch*. When Wilhelm died, they had only reached the letter "D", and the massive project was not finally completed until 1961.

Jacob never married, but in 1825 Wilhelm married Dortchen Wild, from whom, when she was a girl, the brothers had recorded several stories, including "Rumpelstiltskin", "Manyfurs", and "Mother Snow". Dortchen was, like many of the Grimms' sources, a middle-class girl; she was probably remembering the tales from the telling of her nurse.

The most famous of all the storytellers who contributed to the Grimms' collection was Dorothea Viehmann, from the village of Niederzwehren, near Cassel. The Grimms collected more than twenty tales from her, including "Clever Elsie", "The Peasant's Wise Daughter", "Hans the Hedgehog", "The Three Lazybones", and "The Miller's Boy and the Cat". Wilhelm called her the "fairytale-wife", and wrote, "She tells her stories with care, confidence and great vitality, and enjoys doing so." Frau Viehmann was perhaps the most authentic folk storyteller among the Grimms' known sources; although John M. Ellis implies that her repertoire derived from the French stories of Charles Perrault, this is not true.

Another valued storyteller was the retired sergeant of dragoons Friedrich Krause, who told the Grimms the cheerfully amoral tale of "The Knapsack, the Hat and the Horn" in exchange for an old pair of trousers.

One other story has a particularly interesting origin. The comic tale of "The Fisherman and His Wife", which is echoed in the first part of "The Gold Children", was collected by the Romantic painter Philipp Otto Runge, who recorded it in Pomeranian dialect. The wonderful descriptive detail in this well-rounded story may owe something to Runge's painter's eye. Recently Brian Alderson has translated this tale into Yorkshire dialect, and

Gilbert McKay into Scots. Both these versions are well worth searching out –
Alderson's in *The Brothers Grimm: Popular Folk Tales* (1978) and McKay's
in *Jacob and Wilhelm Grimm: Selected Tales*, edited by David Luke (1982).

Whatever their sources, the Grimms' stories live in our minds because they
take us deep into the fairy-tale world in which wishes come true, and the
humble and the generous triumph over the mean and the proud. This is a
world whose rules and customs the brothers Grimm well understood, and in
which, thanks to their work, we can live happily for all our days.

NEIL PHILIP

THE
FAIRY TALES

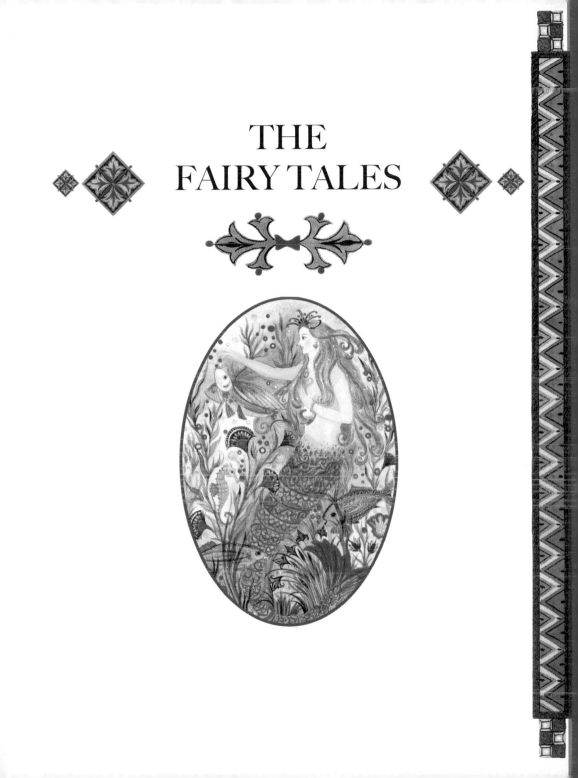

THE
FROG PRINCE

In the old days, when wishing still helped, there lived a king whose daughters were all beautiful, but the youngest was so beautiful that even the sun, who has seen so much, was amazed when he shone on her face.

Not far from the palace there was a great, dark forest, and under an old lime tree in the forest there was a spring. On hot days, the youngest princess used to go into the forest and sit beside the cool water, and when she was bored she took a golden ball and threw it into the air and caught it. It was her best-loved toy.

Now one day it so happened that the princess missed the ball, and it rolled into the spring. All the princess could do was watch it as it sank under the water and disappeared, for the spring was deep, so deep you couldn't see the bottom.

The princess began to cry. Her sobs grew louder and louder; she was in such distress. As she cried, she heard a voice saying,

"What's the matter, king's daughter? You are crying so hard, even a stone would pity you."

She looked where the voice was coming from, and saw a frog sticking its big ugly head out of the water.

"Oh! It's you, is it, splish-splash?" she said. "I am crying because my golden ball has fallen into the spring."

"Hush then, don't cry," said the frog. "I can help you. But what will you give me if I bring you back your toy?"

"Anything you like, you dear frog," she replied. "My clothes, my pearls, my jewels, even my golden crown."

"What do I care for your clothes, your pearls, your jewels, or your golden crown?" said the frog. "But if you will let me be your friend, and sit with you at the table, and eat from your golden plate, and drink from your golden cup, and sleep in your bed, then I will dive down and fetch your golden ball."

"Oh yes," she said. "I promise!" But secretly she thought, *What nonsense this silly frog talks. All he does is sit in the water and croak. How could he be my friend?*

Once she had promised, the frog disappeared under the water and soon came back with the golden ball in its mouth and threw it on the grass.

The princess was so happy to have her toy back. She picked it up and ran off with it. The frog cried, "Wait! Take me with you. I can't run like you!" But no amount of croaking could make the princess listen. She was hurrying home and had already forgotten about the poor frog.

Next day, when the princess sat down at the table with the king and all the courtiers, and was eating from her golden plate, something came hopping, splish-splash, splish-splash, up the marble steps. When it came to the top, it knocked at the door, crying, "Princess, youngest princess, let me in."

She ran to see who was outside, and when she opened the door, she saw the frog. She slammed the door shut as fast as she could and sat down again. Her heart was beating so fast. The king could see she was scared. He said, "What are you afraid of, child? Is there a giant outside who wants to carry you off?"

"It's not a giant," she said. "It's a nasty, slimy frog."

"What does the frog want with you?"

"Oh, Father dear, yesterday when I was in the forest sitting by the spring, my golden ball fell into the water. Because I cried so, the frog fetched it out for me, but first it made me promise it could live with me and be my friend. I never thought it could get out of the spring, but now it's outside and wants to come in."

As they were speaking, the frog knocked a second time, calling,

> *Princess, youngest princess,*
> *Let me in.*
> *You gave me your promise,*
> *Down by the spring.*
> *Princess, youngest princess,*
> *Let me in.*

Then the king said, "You must keep your promises. Go and let it in." She went and opened the door and the frog hopped in and followed her, splish-splash, back to her chair.

Then the frog called, "Lift me up beside you." She didn't know what to do, but the king told her to lift it up.

Once he was on the chair, the frog said, "Push your golden plate nearer, so that we can eat together." With a bad grace, she did as he asked. The frog enjoyed his food, but every mouthful stuck in her throat.

At last the frog said, "I have eaten enough. Now I am tired, so carry me to your room and prepare your silken bed. Then we'll lie down and sleep."

The princess began to cry, because she was afraid of the cold frog. She didn't want to touch it, yet it wanted to sleep in her pretty, clean bed.

The king said angrily, "He helped you when you were in trouble, so you mustn't despise him now."

So she picked up the frog between the tips of two fingers, carried him upstairs, and dropped him in the corner. She got into bed and pulled the covers up tight, but the frog hopped, splish-splash, across the room, calling, "I'm tired, and I want to sleep in your bed. Lift me up or I shall tell your father."

She was so angry, she lifted the frog in both hands and hurled it against the wall. "That should shut you up, you horrible frog," she said.

But when the frog fell to the floor, he wasn't a frog anymore. He was a handsome prince with sparkling eyes. And it was her father's will that he should be her husband.

"A wicked witch put a spell on me," he said, "and only you could have broken it. Sleep now, and tomorrow I shall take you to my kingdom."

In the morning, a carriage arrived, drawn by eight white horses with golden harnesses, and ostrich plumes in their headbands. Behind them stood faithful Henry, the young prince's servant.

Faithful Henry had been so sad when his master was turned into a frog that he had had three iron bands forged around his heart, to stop it from bursting with grief. Now he had come in the carriage to take his master home. He helped the prince and princess into the carriage and stepped up behind them, full of joy.

After they had driven part of the way, the prince heard a great *crack*! He turned around, saying, "Henry, the carriage is breaking."

"No, master, it is an iron band that I had forged around my heart to keep it from breaking when you were turned into a frog and imprisoned in the spring."

Twice more on their journey the prince heard a *crack*! Twice more he thought the carriage was breaking. But it was only faithful Henry's heart filling with happiness, and snapping the iron bands of sorrow.

THE TINDERBOX

L *eft, right! Left, right!*

A soldier came marching down the road. He had a pack on his back and a sword at his side. He was coming home from the wars.

On the way he met an old witch. She was so ugly, her lower lip hung right down to her chest. "Good evening, handsome," she said. "I can see from your pack and your sword that you are a real soldier. How would you like to be rich?"

"I'd like it very much, old witch," said the soldier.

"Do you see that big tree over there?" said the witch, pointing to a tree nearby. "It's quite hollow inside. If you climb to the top, you can get in and lower yourself to the bottom. I'll tie a rope around your waist so I can pull you back up when you call."

"Why should I do that?" asked the soldier.

"To fetch the treasure!" said the witch. "Now, listen. When you get to the bottom you will find yourself in a wide passage lit by over a hundred lamps. You will see three doors, with keys in the locks. If you go through the first door you will see a large chest, guarded by a dog with eyes as big as saucers. But don't worry about him! I'll lend you my blue-and-white checked apron.

Just spread it on the floor, and lift the dog down off the chest and onto the apron. Then you can open the chest and take out as many coins as you like. But they're only coppers. If you want silver, you'll have to go through the second door.

"Behind that is a dog with eyes as big as soup plates. But don't mind him! Just put him on the apron, and take the money.

"Or if you'd prefer gold, go through the third door. The dog in there is a bit of a caution – eyes as big as cartwheels! But don't worry. Just put him on the apron and he won't hurt you. Then you can take as much gold as you can carry."

"That's all very well," said the soldier, "but what do you get out of it, witch? I've no doubt you'll want your cut."

"No," said the witch, "I won't take a single penny. All I want is an old tinderbox, for its sentimental value. My granny left it behind by mistake last time she was down there."

"Let's get on with it then," said the soldier. "Tie the rope around my waist."

"There you are," said the witch, "and here is the apron."

So the soldier climbed the tree and lowered himself down the hole in the trunk, until he came to the wide passage lit by over a hundred lamps, just as the witch had promised.

He opened the first door. Oh! There was the dog with eyes as big as saucers, glaring at him.

"Good dog!" he said. He set it down on the witch's apron, opened the chest, and took as many copper coins as he could cram into his pockets. Then he shut the chest and lifted the dog back onto it.

He opened the second door. Ah! There was the dog with eyes as big as soup plates. "Don't stare at me like that!" said the soldier. "You'll strain your eyes." And he set the dog down on the apron. When he saw all the silver coins in the chest, he threw away the copper ones and filled his pockets and his pack with silver.

He opened the third door. Ugh! There was the dog with eyes as big as cartwheels – and they were spinning round in his head!

"Good evening," said the soldier, and he saluted, for he had never seen such a dog in his life. For a while the soldier just stood there looking at him, but then he said to himself, *Enough of this!* and lifted the dog down onto the apron.

When he opened the chest – my goodness what a lot of gold there was! Enough to buy up the whole city of Copenhagen, and all the gingerbread men and tin soldiers and rocking horses in the world. There was an absolute fortune.

So the soldier cast aside the silver coins and filled his pockets and his pack with gold instead; he even stuffed it down his boots and in his cap. He could hardly move – but he was rich!

He put the dog back on the chest, slammed the door behind him, and called up through the hollow tree, "Pull me up, you old witch!"

"Have you got the tinderbox?" asked the witch.

"No," said the soldier, "I'd clean forgotten it." He went back to fetch it, and then the witch hauled him up. Then he was standing back on the road, with his pockets and his pack, his boots and his cap filled with gold.

"What's so special about the tinderbox?" he asked.

"Mind your own business," snapped the witch. "You've got your money. Just give me the box."

"Stuff and nonsense!" said the soldier. "Tell me what it's for or I'll cut off your head."

"No!" said the witch.

So he cut off her head. There she lay!

The soldier bundled up all his gold in her apron and slung it over his shoulder, tucked the tinderbox in his pocket, and set off to town.

It was a fine town, and the soldier checked into the finest hotel in the place. He stayed in the best rooms and ordered the choicest things on the menu, because now he was a rich man with money to burn.

The servant who cleaned his boots did think it was odd that such a wealthy man should have such shabby shoes – for the soldier hadn't had time to buy anything yet. But next day the soldier kitted himself out with smart clothes and new boots, and then he really looked the part of a fashionable gentleman. Everyone wanted to know him. They boasted to him about their town, and about their king and his beautiful daughter.

"I'd like to see her," said the soldier.

"No one can see her," they answered. "She lives in a copper castle surrounded by walls and towers. The king doesn't let anyone in to see her, because it was foretold that she will marry a common soldier, and the king doesn't like that idea at all."

Wouldn't I like to get a look at her! thought the soldier, but it was no use thinking of that.

His life now was a merry one. And when he went to the theatre, or out riding in his carriage, he gave away lots of money to the poor, because he remembered when his own pockets had been empty.

Now that he was rich and well dressed, he had many friends. They all told him how generous he was, and that this was the mark of a true gentleman, and the soldier liked that. But as he was spending money like water and never earning any more, he was soon down to his last two coppers. He had to leave his fine suite and move to a poky little room in the attic. Now he had to polish his own boots and darn his own clothes. None of his new friends ever came to see him; they said there were too many stairs to climb.

One evening he was sitting in the dark, without even a candle, when he remembered that he had seen a candle stub in the tinderbox when he fetched it out of the tree for the old witch. So he got out the candle stub, and struck a spark from the tinderbox.

As soon as he had done so, the door sprang open, and there was the dog with eyes as big as saucers, saying, "What is your command, master?"

What's going on here! thought the soldier. *This is a funny sort of tinderbox. Can I have whatever I want!* And he said to the dog, "Bring me some money!" It was gone and back in a flash, and when it returned it was carrying a big sack of copper coins in its mouth.

Now the soldier began to appreciate what a special tinderbox it was. If he struck it once it summoned the dog who guarded the copper coins; twice, the dog who guarded the silver; three times, the dog who guarded the gold.

So the soldier was able to move back into his old rooms and buy more fine clothes, and all his friends remembered him and took up with him just where they had left off.

One night he was sitting by himself and thinking about the princess. *It's a shame that no one can see her. It doesn't matter how lovely she is if she's kept hidden away in that copper castle. If only I could see her!* And then he thought, *Where's that tinderbox!*

He struck a spark, and the dog with eyes as big as saucers came. "I know it's the middle of the night," the soldier said, "but all the same I'd like to see the princess, if only for a minute."

Away went the dog, and before the soldier could think things over he had returned with the sleeping princess lying on his back. Anyone could see she was a true princess, she was so beautiful. The soldier kissed her. He couldn't help himself – he was a real soldier.

The dog ran straight back to the copper castle with the princess. At breakfast next morning she told her father and mother about the strange dream she had had. "I was riding on a dog's back, and a soldier kissed me."

The queen pursed her lips. "A nice kind of dream that is!" she said. And she insisted that one of her ladies-in-waiting must watch over the princess that night, just in case.

The soldier longed to see the princess again, and so that night he sent the dog to fetch her. And although the dog was very fast, the old lady who was watching over the princess had just time to pull on her boots and run after it. She saw the dog go into a big house. *Aha!* she thought. She chalked a white cross on the door, so that she would be able to find it in the morning. Then she went home to bed.

When the dog carried the princess back to the castle, he noticed the white cross on the soldier's door. So the dog took some chalk and put a cross on every door in town. It was a clever thing to do, because now the lady-in-waiting would never find the right door.

The next morning the king and the queen, the old lady-in-waiting and all the court went out to see where the princess had been. "Here it is!" exclaimed the king, when he saw a door with a cross in it.

"No, it's here, dear," said the queen, who had seen another door with a cross.

"Here's one!"

"Here's another!"

Wherever they looked, every door had a cross. So they gave up. But the queen had quick wits; she was good for more than just riding around in a carriage. She took her gold scissors and cut out some silk and sewed it into a pretty bag, which she filled with fine white flour. That evening, she tied the bag to the princess's waist and then made a tiny hole in it with her scissors, so that if the princess moved, flour would leak out.

That night the dog came once more to fetch the princess. The soldier loved her so. How he wished he were a prince so that he could marry her.

The dog never noticed the flour, which made a trail all the way from the castle to the soldier's room. So in the morning the king and queen could see where their daughter had been taken. They had the soldier arrested and thrown into prison.

And there he sat in the dark, with nothing to do but listen to them saying, "You'll be hanged tomorrow!" It wasn't much fun. And what's worse, the tinderbox had been left behind at the hotel.

In the morning, the soldier looked through the iron bars of his cell and watched the people going out of town to the place where the gallows had been set up. The royal guards marched past to the sound of drums. Everyone was in a hurry to see him hanged.

Last of all was a shoemaker's apprentice, in his leather apron and slippers. As he cantered along, one of his slippers fell off and landed right outside the soldier's window.

"Hey!" shouted the soldier. "Apprentice! Not so fast! They can't start without me. If you will go to my room and fetch me my tinderbox, and be quick about it, I'll give you four coppers."

The shoemaker's apprentice was very glad of the chance to earn four coppers, so he sprinted off at the double to fetch the tinderbox and bring it back to the soldier.

And now you shall hear what happened then.

The gallows had been set up outside the town gates, and all the guards and the people were standing around it. The king and the queen were sitting on their thrones opposite the judge and the whole council.

The soldier had climbed the ladder, and the executioner was just about to fasten the noose around his neck. Then the soldier spoke up. He said it was the custom to grant a condemned man's last request; all he wanted was to smoke one last pipe of tobacco.

The king couldn't say no to that. So the soldier took his tinderbox and struck it – once, twice, three times! And there stood all three dogs: the one with eyes as big as saucers, the one with eyes as big as soup plates and the one with eyes as big as cartwheels.

"Help me now. I don't want to be hanged!" shouted the soldier. And the dogs fell on the judge and the councillors, tossing them high into the air – so high that when they fell back to the ground, they broke into pieces.

"Not me!" shrieked the king, but the biggest dog picked up both the king and the queen and flung them up into the air like the others.

The royal guards were frightened out of their wits, and the people shouted, "Little soldier, you shall be our king, and marry the princess!"

The soldier sat in the king's carriage, and the three dogs danced in front of it and barked, "Hurrah!" The guards presented arms, while little boys whistled through their fingers.

So the princess left her copper castle and became queen, which she liked much better. The wedding feast lasted for a week, and the dogs sat at the table, staring about them with their great glaring eyes.

RAPUNZEL

There was once a man and a woman who longed in vain for a child. But at last it seemed as if God would answer their prayer.

From the window at the back of their house they could see a wonderful garden full of beautiful flowers and herbs. It was surrounded by a high wall, and no one dared go into it because it belonged to a powerful witch, and everyone was afraid of her.

One day the wife was standing by this window and looking down into the garden, when she caught sight of a lovely bed of rapunzel, which is a kind of lettuce. It looked so fresh and green it made her mouth water. Her craving for the rapunzel grew every day. It was so frustrating to be able to see it but never to eat it that she began to waste away. When her husband saw her so pale and wan, he asked, "What's wrong, darling?"

"Oh," she answered, "if I can't eat some of that rapunzel I shall die."

Her husband loved her, and he thought, *Sooner than let my wife die, I shall get her some of that rapunzel, whatever the cost.*

As dusk fell, he climbed over the wall into the witch's garden, snatched a handful of rapunzel, and took it to his wife. She made it into a salad straightaway and ate it greedily. It tasted good to her – so very good. The next day her craving was three times as great. It wouldn't let her rest.

There was nothing for it. The husband had to go back to the witch's garden. At dusk, he climbed the wall again. But when he came down on the other side, he nearly jumped out of his skin. There stood the witch, right in front of him!

She glared at him. "How dare you sneak into my garden and steal my rapunzel! I'll make you wish you hadn't."

"Have mercy," he pleaded. "I had to do it. My wife saw the rapunzel from our window, and she felt such a craving for it that she would have died if she hadn't got some to eat."

The witch's face softened. "If that's the case, I will let you pick as much rapunzel as you like, on one condition. When your wife's baby is born, you must give it to me. I will look after it and love it like a mother."

The man was so frightened he would have agreed to anything.

So when the baby was born, the witch came and took it away. It was a baby girl, and the witch called her Rapunzel.

Rapunzel grew into the most beautiful child under the sun. When she was twelve years old, the witch took her into the forest and shut her up in a tower that had neither stairs nor door, but only a little window right at the top. When the witch wanted to come in, she stood beneath it and called,

> *Rapunzel, Rapunzel,*
> *Let down your hair.*

Rapunzel had wonderful long hair, as fine as spun gold. When she heard the witch calling, she undid her braided tresses and let them tumble all the way to the ground so that the witch could climb up them.

A few years later, it happened that a prince was passing through the forest and rode by the tower. From it, he heard someone singing. It was Rapunzel, who often sang to herself. Her voice was so lovely and haunting that the prince stopped to listen. He wanted to climb up to her, but when he looked for the door to the tower, he could not find one. He rode away, but the singing had moved him so much that he came back every day to listen to it.

Once, when the prince was standing listening to Rapunzel's singing, the witch came. He heard her call,

> *Rapunzel, Rapunzel,*
> *Let down your hair.*

Then Rapunzel let down her tresses, and the witch climbed up to her.

Aha! he thought. *If that is the ladder by which I can climb up to her, then I will try my luck.* Next day, as dark fell, he went to the tower and called,

> *Rapunzel, Rapunzel,*
> *Let down your hair.*

The hair fell down, and he climbed up.

At first Rapunzel was terrified. She had never seen a man before. But the prince spoke so gently to her that she lost her fear. He said, "My heart was so moved by your singing that I could not rest. Please marry me."

He was so young and handsome, and Rapunzel thought he would love her more truly than the old witch. "Yes," she said. "I will marry you." And she gave him her hand.

Then Rapunzel said, "But how will I ever get down? . . . I know. Every

time you come, you must bring a skein of silk, and then I can make a ladder with it. When it's finished, I will climb down, and you can carry me off on your horse." They agreed that until that time, he should visit her every evening, for the old witch always came in the day.

The old witch suspected nothing, until one day Rapunzel wondered aloud, "Why are you so much heavier to pull up than the prince? He is up in a moment."

"You wicked child!" screeched the witch. "What did you say? I thought I had shut you away from the world, but you have tricked me!" She was so angry that she took a pair of scissors and cut off all Rapunzel's beautiful hair. *Snip-snap* went the scissors, and the lovely tresses fell to the floor. Then the pitiless witch sent Rapunzel into the desert to live in grief and want.

That evening, the witch fastened the severed tresses to the window latch, and when the prince called,

> *Rapunzel, Rapunzel,*
> *Let down your hair,*

she let the hair down. The prince climbed up, but instead of his dear Rapunzel he found the witch, who fixed him with her evil eyes.

"Ah!" she said. "Your lovebird has flown. She is no longer singing in her nest. And she won't be singing anymore. The cat has taken her, and she'll scratch your eyes out too. You've lost Rapunzel. You'll never see her again."

The prince was in an agony of grief. In despair he leaped from the tower. His fall was broken by brambles, but the thorns scratched his eyes and left him blind.

The prince wandered blindly through the forest, living on roots and berries, and weeping and wailing over the loss of his dear wife.

He wandered in misery like this for several years, until at last he came to the desert where Rapunzel was living a wretched existence with the twins she had borne – a boy and a girl. He heard a voice that seemed familiar, and approached it. Rapunzel recognized him at once and flung herself weeping around his neck.

Two of Rapunzel's tears fell on his eyes, and gave him back his sight.

He took her back to his kingdom. They were welcomed with great rejoicing and lived happily together for many years to come.

THE
LITTLE
MERMAID

F ar out to sea the water is as blue as the petals of the loveliest
cornflower and as clear as the purest glass; but it is deep, deeper than
any anchor can reach. Countless church steeples would
have to be piled one on top of the other to stretch from the sea bed to the
surface. That's where the sea folk live.

Now you mustn't imagine that the bottom is just bare white sand; not at
all. Wonderful trees and plants grow down there, with stems and leaves so
sensitive that they curl and sway with the slightest movement of the water, as
if they were living creatures. Fish, large and small, flit through the branches
just like birds in the air up here.

At the very deepest point lies the palace of the sea king. Its walls are of
coral, and the long, pointed windows are of the clearest amber. The roof is
made of cockle shells that open and shut with the play of the waves. It's
lovely to see, because nestling in each shell is a shining pearl, anyone of
which would be the pride of a queen's crown.

The sea king had been a widower for many years, but his old mother kept
house for him. She was a wise old lady, but rather too proud of being royal;
that's why she always wore twelve oysters on her tail, when the rest of the

nobility were only allowed six. Aside from that she was a praiseworthy sort, and she took very good care of her granddaughters, the little sea princesses.

There were six of them, all beautiful, but the youngest was the loveliest of them all. Her skin was pure and clear as a rose petal, and her eyes were as blue as the deepest lake. But like all the others, she had no legs – her body ended in a fish's tail.

All the livelong day they would play down there in the palace, in its spacious apartments where living flowers grew from the walls. When the great amber windows were open, the fish would dart in and out, just as swallows do up here, and they would eat out of the princesses' hands and let themselves be petted.

Outside the castle was a great park with trees of deep blue and fiery red; their fruits shone like gold, and their flowers glowed like flames among the flickering leaves. The earth was of the finest sand, but blue as burning sulphur. Everything was suffused with blue, so that you might think you were high up in the air, with sky above and below you, rather than down at the bottom of the sea. When the sea was calm, you could glimpse the sun up above, like a crimson flower from which light came streaming down.

Each little princess had her own patch of garden, where she could plant whatever she fancied. One made a flowerbed in the shape of a whale; another preferred hers to look like a mermaid. But the youngest princess made hers round like the sun and would only plant flowers that shone red like it. She was a strange child, quiet and thoughtful. Her sisters' gardens were full of oddments salvaged from shipwrecks, but she had only the statue of a handsome boy in hers. It was carved from clear white marble, and it had sunk to the bottom of the sea when the ship that was carrying it was lost. Beside this statue she planted a rose-red weeping willow, which grew taller than it and shaded it with its overhanging branches. In the play of violet shadows on

the blue sand, it looked as if the statue and the tree were embracing.

The princesses liked nothing more than to listen to stories of the world above. The old grandmother had to tell again and again everything she knew about ships, and towns, and people, and animals. The youngest princess was particularly taken with the idea that up above flowers were scented, for at the bottom of the sea they had no smell at all. She also liked to hear about the green forest, and how the fish that swam among the branches could sing so beautifully. Her grandmother called birds "fish" – otherwise the princesses wouldn't have understood, for they had never seen a bird.

"When you turn fifteen," their grandmother would say, "you too will be able to swim to the surface and sit on rocks in the moonlight to watch the great ships sailing by. If you dare, you can swim close enough to the shore to see woods and towns."

The following year the oldest of the sisters would be fifteen. The others were each spaced about a year apart, so that the youngest would have to wait another five whole years before she was allowed to swim up from the sea bed and take a look at us. But each sister promised the others she would come back after her first day on the surface and tell all the exciting things she had seen. For their grandmother didn't tell them nearly enough – there was so much they wanted to know.

None of them was so full of yearning as the youngest – the one who had the longest time to wait, and who was so quiet and thoughtful. Many a night she stood at the open window and gazed up through the dark blue water. She could make out the moon and the stars, though they were pale and blurry beneath the sea. If a black cloud passed over, she knew it must be either a whale swimming overhead or else a ship sailing along the surface; the passengers and crew never dreaming that a lovely mermaid stood in the depths below them and stretched her white hands out to them.

Now the oldest sister was fifteen, and free to swim up to the surface. When she came back she had hundreds of things to tell. The loveliest thing of all, she said, was to lie in the moonlight on a sandbank when the sea was calm and look across to a seaport town, with its lights twinkling like stars, and music playing, and all the clatter of carts and people; she loved to watch and listen, and to see the church spires and hear the bells ringing. Though she knew she could never go there, yet her heart was filled with longing to.

The youngest princess hung on her every word. Late in the evening, as she stood dreaming at the open window and gazing up through the water, she thought so hard about the town that she imagined she could hear the church bells chime.

Next year the second sister got her freedom. She surfaced just as the sun was setting, and the sight was so ravishing she could barely describe it. The whole sky had been a blaze of gold, she said, and as for the clouds   she couldn't find words to capture their beauty as they sailed over her head, streaked with crimson and violet. A skein of wild swans had flown into the setting sun, as if drawing a white veil across the water. She had swum after them, but as the sun sank, so the vision of sea, sky and cloud had faded.

The third of the sisters was the most daring of them all. She swam right inland up a broad river. She saw green hills covered with vines, castles and farms hidden in the forest. She heard the birds singing, and the sun was so hot that she was often forced to dive back under water to cool her burning face. In a small cove she had come upon a group of human children splashing in the water, quite naked; but when she tried to play with them, they ran off in alarm. Then a little black animal – it was a dog, but she didn't know that – had come and barked at her so furiously that she took fright and headed out to sea. But she would never forget those magnificent woods and green hills, and those sweet little children who tried to swim in the water even though they had no tails.

The fourth sister was not so bold. She stayed well away from shore, and she said that there wasn't anything more beautiful than the open sea, with nothing for miles around and the sky above like a great glass bell. She had seen ships, but so far away they looked like seagulls. She had swum with the dolphins, who had turned somersaults for her, and the huge whales had sprayed jets of water into the air, like so many fountains.

The fifth sister's birthday fell in winter, so she saw something none of her sisters had seen. The sea looked quite green, and great icebergs were floating in it. They looked like pearls, yet each one was larger than a church tower. They had the strangest shapes, and they sparkled like diamonds. She had seated herself on one of the largest, and all the sailors had steered away in fear as they sailed past the iceberg where she sat with her long hair streaming in the wind. By evening a storm was blowing. The dark waves lifted the icebergs high up, and lightning flashed red on the ice. The ships had furled their sails and waited out the storm in terror, while she sat calmly on her iceberg and watched the blue lightning zigzag into the glittering sea.

The first time any of the sisters was allowed to go to the surface she was always delighted to see so many things that were new and beautiful. But when they were older and could go any time they liked, they soon lost interest; they wanted to be back home. The bottom of the ocean was the most beautiful place of all.

Still, many an evening the five sisters would link arms and rise to the surface together. They had lovely voices – more hauntingly beautiful than any human voice – and when a storm was blowing and they thought ships might be wrecked, they would swim in front of them and sing about all the wonders waiting at the bottom of the sea. Their song told the sailors not to be afraid of coming down – but the sailors could not make out the words in the howling storm. Nor did they ever see any of the delights of which the princesses sang, for when the ship sank the crew were drowned, and they came only as dead men to the palace of the sea king.

When the sisters floated up to the surface like this, arm in arm, their little sister stayed behind all alone. As she watched them go she would have cried, but a mermaid has no tears, and so she suffers all the more.

"If only I were fifteen!" she sighed. "I know that I shall love the world up there, and the people who live in it."

And then at last she was fifteen.

"There now! We're getting you off our hands at last," said her old grandmother. "Let me dress you up like your sisters." She set a garland of white lilies in her hair; each petal was half a pearl. Then she made eight big oysters pinch fast onto her tail, to show that she was a princess.

"Ow! That hurts," said the little mermaid.

"One must suffer to be beautiful," said her grandmother.

The little mermaid would have gladly swapped her heavy garland of pearls for some of the red flowers from her garden, which suited her much better, but she didn't dare.

"Goodbye," she said, and she floated up through the water as lightly as a bubble.

The sun had just set when she lifted her head above the water. The clouds still gleamed rose and gold, and in the pale pink sky the evening star shone clear and bright. The air was soft and fresh, and the sea was perfectly calm. A large three-masted ship lay close by. Only one sail was set, because there wasn't a breath of wind. The sailors were sitting idly in the rigging; below on the deck there was music and singing, and as the evening grew dark, hundreds of lanterns were lit, like so many flags.

The little mermaid swam to a porthole and the waves lifted her up so that she could see the smartly dressed people inside. The handsomest of all was a

51

young prince with jet-black eyes. This was his sixteenth birthday, and that was the cause of the celebrations. The sailors were dancing up on the deck, and when the young prince appeared, a hundred rockets shot up into the sky and turned the night back into bright day.

The little mermaid was quite scared and ducked back beneath the water, but she soon surfaced again. It felt as if the stars were falling out of the sky. She had never seen such fireworks. Great suns were spinning around, fiery fish were darting about the blue air and all this glitter was reflected back from the clear mirror of the sea. The deck of the ship was so brightly lit that you could see every rope. How handsome the young prince was! He was laughing and smiling and shaking hands with everyone, while music rang out into the night.

It grew late, but the little mermaid could not take her eyes from the ship, and the handsome prince. The lanterns were put out; the rockets were finished; no more cannons were fired. Yet deep beneath the sea there was a murmuring and grumbling. Still the mermaid rocked up and down on the waves to look into the cabin.

The ship gathered speed; more sails were unfurled. The waves became choppy, and clouds began to mass; in the distance there were flashes of lightning. A storm was brewing.

The sails were taken in, and the ship was tossed about by the huge waves that rose like black mountains high above the masts. The ship was like a swan diving down into the troughs of the waves and riding high on their crests. The little mermaid watched it all with glee – she thought it was great fun. But it was no joke for the sailors. The ship creaked and cracked, and its stout timbers shivered as the raging sea pounded against them. Suddenly the main mast snapped like a stick, and then the ship keeled over on her side as water poured into the hold.

Now the little mermaid could see that they were in danger; she herself had to watch out for planks and bits of wreckage that were floating in the water. For a moment it was so dark she couldn't see a thing; then lightning flashed and she could make out all the figures on board. It was every man for himself. She looked desperately for the young prince, and caught sight of him just as the ship broke up and sank into the sea. For a split second she was filled with joy. Now he was coming to her! But then she remembered that men cannot live in the water, and that he could only come to her father's palace as a corpse.

No! He must not die! She flung herself forwards, heedless of the drifting beams that might have crushed her, plunging into the turbulent waves again and again until she found the prince. He was barely able to keep afloat in that heaving sea; his arms and legs were tired out. He closed his beautiful eyes, and he must certainly have drowned if the little mermaid had not come to him. She held his head above water and let the waves carry the two of them where they would.

By morning the storm was over. Not a trace of the ship remained. The sun rose up red and glorious from the waves, and it seemed to bring a touch of life to the pale face of the prince, though his eyes remained shut. The mermaid kissed his forehead and stroked his wet hair. She thought he looked like the marble statue in her garden. She kissed him again, and wished with all her heart that he might live.

Now she could see dry land ahead, and high blue mountains with snow-covered peaks. Down by the shore there were green woods and a little whitewashed church or monastery, the little mermaid didn't know which. Orange and lemon trees grew in the garden, and by the gate were tall palms. There was a little bay with deep water right up to the shore, and the mermaid swam into it with the handsome prince and laid him on the white sand in the sun, taking care that his head was out of the water.

Now bells rang out from the building, and some young girls came out to walk in the garden. So the little mermaid swam out to some foam-flecked rocks and hid behind them, so that she could wait for someone to come and help the poor prince.

Quite soon a young girl came by. She seemed startled to see the half-drowned figure, but only for a few seconds; then she went and fetched help. The mermaid saw the prince revive and smile at those around him. He did not smile at her; he did not even know that she had rescued him. She felt empty. After he had been taken into the white building, she dived down into the water and returned sorrowing to her father's palace.

She had always been quiet and thoughtful; now she was even more so. Her sisters asked her what she had seen on her first visit to the surface, but she wouldn't say.

On many evenings, and many mornings, she went back to the place where she had left the prince. She saw the fruits in the garden grow ripe and be harvested. She saw the snow melt from the mountaintops, but she never saw the prince, and so she always went home even sadder than before.

Her one comfort was to sit in her little garden with her arms wrapped around the beautiful marble statue that reminded her so much of the prince. She never tended the flowers, and they grew wild and tangled, climbing and interweaving until they shut out all the light from the garden.

At last she could bear it no longer and told one of her sisters her story; so before long all the sisters knew about it — but nobody else, except for a few mermaids who only told their closest friends. And it was one of these who found out who the prince was. She too had seen the birthday party on the ship, and she knew where he came from and where his kingdom lay.

"Come on, little sister," said the other princesses, and with their arms twined around each other's shoulders they rose up through the sea to surface outside the prince's palace.

The palace was built of pale yellow stone, with great flights of marble steps, one of which stretched right down to the sea. Gilded domes capped the roof, and between the pillars around the building were lifelike marble statues. Through the clear glass of the high windows you could see right into the state apartments with their precious hangings and tapestries and wonderful paintings. In the middle of the biggest room a great fountain played, splashing its water right up to a glass dome in the roof. The sun shone down through the glass onto the fountain and the beautiful plants that grew in it.

Now that she knew where he lived, she went there many an evening and many a night. She swam closer than any of the others dared – right up the narrow canal into the shadow cast by the prince's marble balcony. There she would gaze at the young prince, who believed himself all alone in the moonlight.

Often in the evening she saw him sailing in his fine boat, with its banners flying and music playing. She peeped from behind the reeds on the shore, and if anyone caught sight of her long silver veil when it was caught by the breeze, they only thought it was a swan flirting its wings.

Many a time, later at night, when the fishermen were casting their nets by torchlight, she heard them speaking well of the young prince, and that made her glad, for she had saved his life when he lay drifting half-dead on the waves. She remembered how his head had rested on her breast, and how fiercely she had kissed him. But he knew nothing about that; he never dreamed she existed.

She became fonder and fonder of human beings, and longed to join them. Their world seemed so much larger than hers. They could sail across the oceans in ships, and climb mountains high above the clouds.

Their lands with their fields and forests seemed to stretch forever. There was so much she wanted to know; questions her sisters couldn't answer. So she quizzed her old grandmother for everything she knew about the upper world, as she called the countries above the sea.

"If human beings are not drowned, do they live forever?" she asked. "Or do they die, as we do in the sea?"

"Yes," said the old lady, "they must die. And their lives are far shorter than ours. We can live for three hundred years, but at the end we just turn to foam on the water – we do not even have a grave down here among our loved ones. We do not have immortal souls; there is no new life for us. We're like the green reeds – once they are cut, they will never be green again. But human beings have a soul which lives forever, even after their body has turned to dust. The soul rises through the air to the bright stars. Just as we rise up out of the sea and gaze on the upper world, so they rise up to unknown glorious regions that we shall never see."

"Why have we no immortal soul?" the little mermaid asked sadly. "I would give all my three hundred years if I could live as a human being for one single day, and share in that heavenly world."

"You must not think of such things," said her grandmother. "We are happier and better off here than they are up there."

"So I shall die, and drift as foam upon the ocean," said the little mermaid, "and never hear the waves again, or see the lovely flowers and the red sun. Is there nothing I can do to gain an immortal soul?"

"No," said the old lady. "Only if a human loved you more than his father and mother, and thought only of you, and let a priest take his right hand and put it in yours, while he promised to be true to you for all eternity, then his soul would flow into you, and you would share in human happiness. He would give you a soul, yet still keep his own. But that can never be. For what we think beautiful down here – your tail – is thought ugly up there. They prefer two clumsy props, called legs."

The little mermaid glanced down at her fishtail, and sighed.

"We must be content with what we have," said the old lady, "and make the best of our three hundred years. We should dance and be gay; for it's a long sleep after. Tonight, let's have a court ball!"

It was a magnificent affair, the like of which has never been seen on earth. The walls and ceilings of the great ballroom were made of glass – quite thick, but perfectly clear. Several hundred enormous shells, rose red and grass green, were ranged as lamps on either side, and their blue flames lit up the whole room. Light spilled through the glass walls into the sea outside, where countless fish could be seen swimming about, their scales glowing purple, silver and gold.

Through the middle of the ballroom flowed a broad swift stream, on which the sea folk danced to their own sweet songs. No humans have such lovely voices, and the little mermaid sang most beautifully of all. The others clapped their hands for her, and for a moment she felt a thrill of joy, for she knew that she had the most beautiful voice of anyone on land or sea. But her thoughts soon returned to the world above, for she could not forget the handsome prince and her grief that she did not, like him, have an immortal soul. So she crept out of her father's palace, and while everyone else danced and sang, she sat alone in her gloomy little garden.

From up above she heard the sound of a horn echoing through the water. *There he is*, she thought, *sailing so far beyond my reach, though I love him more than my father and mother, though he is always in my thoughts, though I would place my life's happiness in his hands.*

To win his love, and gain an immortal soul, I would dare anything! While my sisters are dancing in the palace, I will go to the sea witch, though I have always feared her, and ask her to help me.

And so the little mermaid left her garden and swam to the place where the sea witch lived, on the far side of a raging whirlpool. She had never gone that way before. No flowers grew there; no sea grass; nothing but bare sand until she reached the fearsome whirlpool, which was twisting and turning like a millwheel, dragging everything it could clutch down into the deep. She had to brave those roaring waters to reach the sea witch's domain. Once through the whirlpool, the path lay over a swamp of hot, bubbling mud, which the sea witch called her peat bog. Beyond this lay the witch's house, deep in an eerie forest.

The trees and bushes in this forest were all what they call polyps – half beast and half plant. They looked like hundred-headed snakes growing from the ground. Their branches were long slimy arms with fingers like wiggling worms; they never stopped moving, from root to tip, and whatever they touched they wound round, never to let go.

The little mermaid paused at the edge of this wood. She was so frightened she thought her heart would stop beating. She almost turned back. But then she thought of the prince, and the human soul, and that gave her courage. She bound up her long flowing hair, so that the polyps could not snatch at it. Then she folded her hands together and dived forward, darting as fast as the fastest fish, in and out of the gruesome branches, which reached out their waving arms after her.

She noticed that every one of them was holding tight to something it had caught: white skulls of drowned men, ships' rudders and seamen's chests, skeletons of land animals, and – most horrible of all – a little mermaid whom they had taken and throttled.

Now she came to a swampy clearing in the wood, where enormous eels were writhing about, exposing their gross, sallow underbellies. Here the

witch had built her house from the bones of shipwrecked men, and here she
sat, letting a toad feed out of her mouth, just as some people do with a pet
canary. She called the vile, slimy eels her little chickabiddies, and pressed
them close to her great spongy chest.

"I know what you're after," she cackled, "and you're a fool. But you shall
have your wish, for it will only bring you misery, my pretty princess. You
want to be rid of your fishtail, and have two stumps instead, like humans
have, and then the prince will fall in love with you, and you will marry him,
and win an immortal soul – isn't that so?" And the sea witch gave such an
evil laugh that the toad and the eels fell away from her and lay there
sprawling in the slime.

"You've come in the nick of time," said the witch. "Tomorrow I couldn't
have helped you for another year. I shall prepare you a potion. Tomorrow
morning go to the shore and drink it before the sun rises. Then your tail will
split in two, and shrink into what humans call "pretty legs". But it will hurt. It
will be like a sharp sword slicing through you. Everyone who sees you will say
you are the loveliest girl they have ever seen. But though you will move with a
dancer's grace, every step you take will be like treading on a sharp knife – a
blade that cuts to the bone. Will you suffer all this! If so, I can help you."

"Yes," said the little mermaid, though her voice trembled. She fixed her
thoughts on the prince, and the prize of an immortal soul.

"Don't forget," said the witch, "when once you have taken a human shape,
you can never again be a mermaid. You can never dive down to your father's
place, or to your sisters. Yet if you do not win the prince's love, so that he
forgets his father and mother and thinks only of you, and lets the priest join
your hands as man and wife, then you will get no immortal soul. On the
morning after the prince marries another, your heart will break and you will
be nothing but foam on the water."

"My mind is made up," said the little mermaid, as pale as death.

"Then there's the matter of my fee," said the witch. "I won't do it for nothing. Yours is the most beautiful voice of all the sea folk; I expect you think to use it to charm the prince. But that voice you must give to me. You must pay for my potion with the most precious thing you possess. For in return I must shed my own blood, to make the potion as sharp as a two-edged sword."

"But if you take my voice," said the little mermaid, "what will I have left?"

"Your beauty, your grace and your speaking eyes," said the witch. "These are enough to win a human heart. Well! Have you lost your courage! Put out your little tongue, and I shall cut it off in payment; then you shall receive my precious potion."

"Let it be so," said the little mermaid.

The witch put a cauldron on the fire to prepare her potion.

"Cleanliness is a good thing," she said, wiping out the cauldron with some eels that she had tied into a knot. Then she scratched her breast and let black blood drip into the cauldron. The steam that arose was full of terrifying shapes. Every moment the witch threw some dread ingredient into the brew. When it came to the boil, it made the sound of a crying crocodile. But when the potion was ready, it looked like the clearest water.

"There you are!" said the witch, and she cut off the little mermaid's tongue. Now she had no voice, and she could neither sing nor speak.

"If the polyps give you any trouble on the way back," said the witch, "just throw one single drop of this potion at them, and they will split apart." But there was no need for that. When the polyps saw her, they shrank back in terror from the bright vial shining in her hand like a star. So the little mermaid passed safely back across the wood, the swamp and the roaring whirlpool.

She could see her father's palace. The lights were out in the great ballroom; everyone must be asleep. She didn't dare go and look, now that she had lost her voice and was going to leave them for ever. She felt her heart would break from grief. She crept into the garden and took one flower from the flower beds of each of her sisters; then she blew them each a farewell kiss, and rose up through the deep blue sea.

The sun had not yet risen when she reached the prince's castle and made her way up the marble steps. The moon shone bright and clear. The little mermaid drank the bitter, burning drink, and it was as if a two-edged sword had been thrust through her delicate body. She fainted away with the pain.

When the sun's rays touched her she awoke. The pain was still as sharp, but there in front of her stood the young prince. He fastened his jet-black eyes on her, and she cast her eyes down – and then she saw that her fishtail was gone, and that instead she had the prettiest, slenderest legs that any girl could wish for. But she was quite naked, so she wrapped herself in her long flowing hair.

The prince asked who she was and how she had come there, but she could only look at him with her sweet, sad eyes; she could not speak.

He took her by the hand and led her into the palace. Just as the witch had warned her, every step was like treading on a knife-edge. But she welcomed the pain. With her hand in the prince's, she felt she was walking on air. Everyone who saw her was charmed by her grace of movement.

She was given a lovely dress of silk and muslin, and everyone agreed she was the most beautiful girl in the palace. But she was mute, and could neither sing nor speak.

Beautiful girls dressed in silk and gold came and performed for the prince and his parents. One of them sang more prettily than the rest, and the prince clapped his hands and smiled at her. It made the little mermaid sad, for she knew that she had once sung far more beautifully. And she thought, *Oh! If only he knew I had sacrificed my voice in order to be with him!*

Next the girls did a delightful dance. When they had finished, the little mermaid lifted her arms and stood on the tips of her toes. Then she began to float across the dance floor, with a grace that had never been seen before. There was such beauty in her movements, and her eyes were so full of feeling, that everyone was enchanted – especially the prince. He called her his little foundling. So she danced on and on, though every time her foot touched the floor she felt she was treading on sharp knives. The prince declared she must never leave him, and she was given a place to sleep outside his door on a velvet cushion.

The prince had a boy's velvet suit made for her, so that she could ride out with him on horseback. They rode through the sweet smelling woods, where green branches brushed their shoulders, and the little birds trilled from among the cool leaves. She climbed high hills by the prince's side, and though her delicate feet bled for all to see, she only laughed, and followed him until they could see the clouds sailing beneath them like a flock of birds setting off for distant lands.

At night in the palace, while the others slept, she would go down the marble steps and cool her poor burning feet in the cold water. Then she would think of her sisters, down in the deep sea.

One night they came, arm in arm, singing the saddest song. She waved to them, and they recognized her at once. They told her how unhappy she had made them all. After that, they visited every night. Once she saw her old grandmother, far out to sea, and once her father, the sea king, with his crown on his head. They stretched out their hands to her, but they did not venture near enough to speak.

Day by day the prince grew more fond of her. But he loved her only as a dear, good child – he never thought of making her his wife. And she had to become his wife, or she could never win an immortal soul. On the day he married another, she would dissolve into foam on the sea.

"Don't you love me best?" her eyes would plead, when he took her in his arms and kissed her lovely brow.

"You really are the dearest creature," the prince would say, "because you have the kindest heart. You are so devoted, and you remind me of a young girl I saw only once, and shall probably never see again. I was on a ship that was wrecked, and the waves carried me to land close to a convent, which was home to many young maidens. The youngest of them all found me on the beach and saved my life. I saw her but twice, no more, yet I know she is the only one I could ever love, and you are so like her that you almost take her place in my heart. She belongs to the temple, but good fortune has sent you to me – we shall never be parted!"

Ah! He does not know that I was the one who saved his life, thought the little mermaid. *He does not know that I was the one who carried him through the waves to the convent, or that I waited in the foam to see if anyone would come, and saw the pretty girl whom he loves better than me.* She gave a deep sigh, for she did not know how to cry. *The girl belongs to the convent, so she will never come out into the world. I am with him every day. I will care for him, and love him and give up my life to him.*

But now people said that the young prince was to be married. He was fitting out a fine ship to go and see the country of another king, but everyone said, "It's not the country, it's the princess he's going to inspect." The little mermaid just shook her head and smiled a secret smile, for she knew the prince's thoughts, and they didn't.

"I shall have to go," he told her. "My parents insist. But they cannot make me marry this princess, however pretty she is. I cannot love her. She will not remind me of the beautiful girl in the temple, as you do. If ever I chose a bride, I should choose you first, my silent foundling with the speaking eyes!" And he kissed her rose-red mouth, played with her long hair and laid his head so near her heart that she was filled with dreams of human happiness and an immortal soul.

"Have you no fear of the sea, my silent child?" he said, as they stood on the deck of the splendid ship that was to take him to the nearby kingdom. He told the little mermaid how the sea could turn in a moment from calm to storm, and of the rare fish in the deep, and the strange sights divers had seen down there. And she smiled at his tales, for she knew better than he what lay beneath the waves.

In the moonlit night, when everyone but the helmsman at the wheel was asleep, she sat on the ship's rail and stared down through the clear water. She thought she saw her father's palace. On the topmost tower her grandmother was perched, with a silver crown on her head, staring up through the swift current at the passing ship. Then her sisters came to the surface, wringing their white hands, and looking at her with despair. She waved to them and smiled; she wanted them to know that all was well with her. But just then the cabin boy came out, and her sisters dived down; all he saw was foam on the water.

Next morning the ship sailed into port. Church bells rang out, and soldiers stood to attention with glittering bayonets. Banners were flying; everyone was on holiday. The prince was invited to one ball or party after another; but nothing was seen of the princess. It was said that she was being educated at a convent, learning how to be royal.

At last she arrived. The little mermaid was waiting for her, eager to judge her beauty. She had to admit that it would be hard to find a lovelier human girl. Her skin was so clear and delicate, and behind long dark lashes she had a pair of baby blue eyes.

'It is you!" cried the prince. "You who saved me when I lay half dead on the shore." And he clasped the blushing princess in his arms.

"Now I am too happy," he told the little mermaid. "My dearest wish – all I ever dared hope for – has been granted. You, whose heart is so true, will share my happiness." And the little mermaid kissed his hand and thought her heart would break. His wedding morning would bring her death; she would be nothing but foam on the sea.

All the church bells rang, and heralds rode through the streets to announce the wedding.

On the altar, silver lamps burned rare oils. The priests swung censers with burning incense. The prince and princess gave each other their hands, and the bishop blessed them. The little mermaid, dressed in silk and gold, held up the train of the bride's dress. But her ears did not hear the music, and her eyes did not see the sacred ceremony. This night would bring her death, and she was thinking of all she had lost.

That evening, the bride and bridegroom went on board ship; cannons were fired, and banners flew. Right on the main deck, a sumptuous tent of scarlet and gold had been set up, with the softest cushions on which the happy pair would rest on that calm, cool night.

The sails swelled in the breeze, and the ship glided across the clear water.

As darkness fell, bright lamps were lit, and the sailors danced jigs and reels on the deck. The little mermaid remembered the first time she had come to the surface, and had spied on just such a scene. Now she, too, whirled in the dance, gliding and soaring as a swallow does when it is pursued. How everyone cheered and clapped! Never before had she danced with such abandon. Sharp knives sliced her tender feet, but she scarcely felt the pain beside the raw wound in her heart. This was the last time she would see him – the handsome prince for whom she had given up her beautiful voice, turned her back on her home and family, and day after day endured pain without end. He had never noticed any of it. This was the last time she would breathe the same air as he, or look upon the deep sea or the starry sky. An everlasting night, without thoughts, without dreams, awaited her – for she had no soul, nor any hope of one.

The merrymaking lasted long into the night. The little mermaid danced and laughed, with the thought of death heavy in her heart. Then the prince kissed his lovely bride, she caressed his dark locks, and arm in arm they retired to their magnificent tent.

The ship was hushed and still; there was only the helmsman standing at the wheel. The little mermaid leaned her white arms on the rail and looked eastwards for the first pink of dawn. The first ray of sun, she knew, would kill her.

Then she saw her sisters rising out of the water. Their faces were pale and grim, and their long lustrous hair no longer streamed in the wind – it had been cut off.

"We have given our hair to the sea witch, so that she would help us to save your life. She has given us this knife. See how sharp it is! Before the sun rises you must plunge it into the prince's heart. When his warm blood splashes over your feet they will join together into a fishtail, and you will be a mermaid once more. You can come down to us and live out your three hundred years before you melt into the salt sea foam. Hurry! Either he or you must die by sunrise. Our old grandmother is grieving; her white hair has fallen out through sorrow, just as ours fell before the scissors of the witch. Kill the prince, and come back to us! Hurry! Do you not see the red streak in the sky? In a few minutes the sun will rise, and then you must die." And with a strange, deep sigh they sank beneath the waves.

The little mermaid drew aside the purple curtain of the tent and saw the beautiful bride asleep, with her head on the prince's breast. She stooped and

kissed his handsome brow, glanced into the sky where the red light of dawn was glowing ever stronger, and looked back to the prince. In his sleep he was calling his bride by name; she alone filled his thoughts. The knife trembled in the mermaid's hand.

She flung it far out to sea. There was a glimmer of red as it fell, as if red drops of blood were splashing up from the water. One last glimpse of the prince through eyes half glazed by death, and she threw herself into the sea; she felt her body dissolving into the foam.

And now the sun came rising from the sea. It rays were so gentle and warm on the cold foam that the little mermaid did not feel the hand of death. She saw the bright sun and, hovering above her, hundreds of bright transparent creatures – she could see through them to the white sails of the ship and the pink clouds in the sky. Their voices were pure melody – so pure that no human ear could hear it, just as no human eye could see them. They had no wings – they were lighter than air. The little mermaid saw that she had become like them, and was floating free above the foam.

"Who are you?" she asked, and she had a voice again – a voice like theirs, so heavenly that no music could ever capture it.

"We are the daughters of the air!" they replied. "A mermaid has no immortal soul, and she can never gain one unless she wins the love of a mortal. Her only chance of eternal life depends upon another. We daughters of the air are not given an immortal soul either, but by good deeds we can make our own soul. We fly to the hot countries, where plague gathers in the sultry air, and blow cool breezes to dispel it. We carry the healing fragrance of flowers to the sick. If for three hundred years we do nothing but good, then we win an immortal soul and a share in mankind's eternal happiness. You, poor little mermaid, have striven with all your heart. You have suffered, and endured, and have raised yourself into the world of the spirits of the air.

Now, by three hundred years of good deeds, you can make yourself an immortal soul."

And the little mermaid raised her translucent arms to the sun, and for the first time she shed a tear.

She heard life and movement from the ship. The prince and the princess were searching for her; they were gazing sadly into the foam, as if they guessed she had flung herself into the sea. Unseen, she kissed the bride's forehead, gave a smile to the prince, and then with the other daughters of the air she ascended to a rose-pink cloud that was sailing by.

"In three hundred years I shall rise like this into the kingdom of heaven," she whispered.

"Maybe even sooner," said one of the others. "We enter unseen into human homes where there are children. Whenever we find a good child, who makes its parents happy and repays their love, it makes us smile with joy, and a year is taken from the three hundred. But if we see a mean and naughty child, then we must weep tears of sorrow, and every tear adds another day to our time of trial."

THE MILLER'S BOY AND THE CAT

There was an old miller who lived in a mill with no wife or child but only three lads who worked for him. After some years, he said, "I'm getting old. All I want to do is sit by the fire. So I've decided to give the mill to one of you. Whoever brings me back the finest horse shall have the mill, so long as he looks after me until I die."

Now two of the boys were sharp enough, but the third was a nincompoop. The other boys made fun of him and said, "What would you do with a mill, stupid?" And he wasn't even sure himself if he would want it.

The three of them set out together, but when they got to a village, the first two told stupid Hans, "You might as well stop here. You'll never get a horse as long as you live." But Hans stayed with them. At nightfall they came to a cave in which they lay down to sleep, but the two smart ones just waited until Hans had dropped off and then sneaked away, leaving him behind. They thought that was very funny – though, as it turned out, the joke was on them.

When the sun rose, Hans woke to find himself alone in the deep cave. He looked around him, and exclaimed, "Heavens, where am I?" He got up, clambered out of the cave, and found himself in the forest. "I'm lost and alone. How will I ever find a horse now?" he moaned.

As he walked along, thinking such thoughts, a little tabby cat came up to him, and said in a friendly way, "'Morning, Hans. What can I do for you?"

"I'm afraid you can't help me," said Hans.

"I know what you're looking for," the cat replied. "You're looking for a fine horse. Well, if you'll come with me and do my bidding for seven years, I will give you the finest horse you ever laid eyes on."

This is a peculiar cat, thought Hans. *I wonder if she's telling the truth.* There was only one way to find out, so Hans agreed to serve the cat for seven years.

The cat took him back to her enchanted castle. All the servants were kittens, who bounded upstairs and downstairs all day, always happy and playful.

In the evening, when Hans and the tabby cat sat down to dinner, three of the kittens made music for them. One played the double bass, another the fiddle, while the third puffed and blew on a trumpet. And after dinner, the tabby cat said, "Hans, will you dance with me?"

Hans said, "No. I've never danced with a pussycat, and I never will."

So the cat told the kittens to show Hans to his room. One of them showed the way with a candle, another took his shoes off, another took his stockings off and another blew out the light. And in the morning they came back and helped him get dressed. One put his stockings on for him, another tied his garters, one brought his shoes, one washed him and another dried his face with her tail. "How soft that is!" he said.

But Hans had his own work to do. Every day he had to chop wood with a silver axe and a silver saw, a copper mallet and silver wedges.

All the time Hans was in the castle he was very well fed and looked after, but he never saw a soul other than the tabby cat and the kittens.

One day, the cat asked Hans to go and mow the meadow and bring in the

hay. She gave him a silver scythe and a gold whetstone, and he set to work. When the haymaking was done, Hans said, "Isn't it time for my reward?"

"You must do one more thing for me first. I want you to build me a little house. Here is everything you need – wood, and tools all of silver."

Hans built the little house, and when he was finished he said, "Now I have done everything you asked, but I still have no horse." The seven years had flown by like so many months.

"Would you like to see my horses?" asked the tabby cat.

"Yes!" said Hans.

So the cat opened the door of the little silver house that Hans had built, and inside there stood twelve horses, so sleek and glossy that his heart jumped for joy. Then the cat gave Hans food and drink, and said, "I will not give you your horse yet. You go home, and I will follow in three days."

The cat showed him the way to the mill, and Hans set out. Now the cat had never given him any new clothes, so he was still in the same old smock he had come in; and after seven years it was dirty and torn, and far too small.

When he reached the mill, the two smart lads were already there, and each of them had brought a horse, though one of the horses was blind and the other was lame. "Where's your horse, stupid?" they crowed.

"It will follow me in three days," he replied, and they fell about laughing.

The miller wouldn't even let Hans come inside, because he was so ragged and filthy. "What if we have guests?" the miller said. "You'd put us to shame." So Hans had to eat on the doorstep, and sleep in the goosehouse on the hard straw.

When he woke up in the morning, the three days had passed. A coach came to the mill, drawn by six shining horses, and a servant was leading a seventh horse, which was for the miller's boy. A beautiful princess stepped out of the coach and went into the mill, and this princess was the tabby cat

75

Hans had served for seven years.

She asked the miller, "Do you have a boy who serves you?"

"Two of the rascals," said the miller, pointing to the two smart lads.

"Isn't there another?"

"Oh, him!" the miller replied. "He's too dirty to come in here; he's in the goosehouse."

"Bring him to me," said the princess. So they fetched him from the goosehouse. He was holding his tattered smock together for modesty's sake. But the princess's servants unpacked splendid clothes for him. They washed him and dressed him, and when they were finished, he looked as handsome as any king.

Then the princess said, "Let me see the horses the other boys brought home." They showed her the blind nag and the lame one. Then the princess told her servants to bring forward the horse that they had brought for Hans. Its coat glistened, and its muscles rippled underneath its skin. When the miller saw it he said, "This is the finest horse that has ever entered this yard."

"That horse belongs to Hans," said the princess. "Then so does the mill," said the miller.

But Hans didn't want the mill now. "You keep it," he said, "and the horse too."

Hans and the princess drove off in the coach and six, and went to live in the little silver house that he had built – only now it was a big castle, and everything in it was made of gold and silver. They were married, and Hans was so rich that he never had to work again.

Which just goes to show that even a nincompoop can get on in the world.

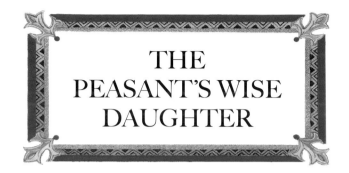

THE PEASANT'S WISE DAUGHTER

There was once a poor peasant who had no land, just a little hut and an only daughter.

One day the daughter said, "We ought to ask the king for a piece of newly cleared land."

When the king heard how poor they were, he gave them a piece of land, which the girl and her father dug over, meaning to sow it with corn and wheat. When they had turned over nearly the whole field, they dug up a mortar made of pure gold.

"Look here," said the father. "As the king was so kind as to give us this field, we ought to give him the golden mortar in return."

The daughter was dead against it. "Father," she said, "if we give the king the golden mortar, he will the demand a golden pestle to go with it, and then what shall we do?" But the old man wouldn't listen.

He took the mortar and presented it to the king. But instead of saying thank you, the king just said, "Are you sure that's all you found?"

"Yes, Your Majesty," said the peasant.

"I don't believe you," said the king. "If you found a golden mortar, you must have found a golden pestle. Bring it to me, or you shall regret it."

The old man protested that he had never seen the golden pestle, but he might as well have saved his breath to cool his porridge. They dragged him off to prison, where he was to stay until he produced the pestle.

The guards who brought him his bread and water couldn't persuade him to eat or drink. All he did was wail, "If only I had listened to my daughter!" They reported this to the king, and the king had the peasant brought before him.

"What do you mean, 'If only I had listened to my daughter'?" asked the king.

"She told me not to give you that mortar, as you would only ask for the pestle as well."

"If you have such a wise daughter, send her to me."

So the peasant's daughter had to appear before the king. He said, "If you are as wise as you seem, I shall marry you. But first you must solve a riddle."

"I will try," said the girl.

The king said, "I want you to come to me neither naked nor clothed, neither riding nor walking, and neither on the road nor off the road. If you can do that, you shall be my queen."

The peasant girl went home and took off all her clothes. Then she wrapped herself in a fishing net, so that she was not naked. Then she hired a donkey and tied the fishing net to the donkey's tail, so that it could pull her along, which was neither riding nor walking. As the donkey pulled her along, it dragged her through the wagon ruts, with only her big toe touching the road. So she was neither on the road nor off the road.

When the king saw the clever way in which she had solved his riddle, he released her father from prison, took her as his wife, and put her in charge of his household.

Some years passed, and then one day as the king was inspecting his troops it happened that two peasants who had been selling wood stopped their wagons outside the palace. One wagon was drawn by two oxen, and the other by two horses. One of the horses had a young foal with it, and this foal ran off and lay down between the oxen. When the foal's owner asked for it back, the other peasant refused, and the two came to blows.

The king wanted to know what the matter was, and the peasants argued their case in front of him. "The foal is mine," said the peasant with the horses. "Nonsense," said the other. "The foal is mine. See how happy it is, lying down between its parents." And the king, who knew nothing about animals, said, "The creature seems happy where it is, so that's where it should stay."

The peasant who had lost his foal didn't dare argue with the king, but he had heard that the queen was kindhearted and came from a peasant family herself, so he took his troubles to her. "Please help me," he begged.

"I will," she said, "if you promise never to betray me. This is what you must do. Tomorrow morning, when the king goes out to inspect the guard, you must stand in the middle of the road with a fishing net and pretend to be fishing in the dust. Every now and then give the net a shake as if it were full, and then carry on." And she also told him what to say when the king spoke to him.

Next day, the king asked him what he thought he was up to. "I'm fishing," he replied.

"How can you catch fish on dry land?" asked the king.

"There's just as much chance of my catching fish on dry land as there is of oxen having a foal."

"You didn't fetch that answer out of your own head," said the king. "Who told you what to say?" But the peasant, because he had promised the queen, would not betray her. The king had him dragged off to prison and beaten and starved until at last he confessed that it was the queen who had advised him what to do and say.

When the king got home, he said to his wife, "You have made me a laughing stock. I won't have you for my wife anymore. You can go back to the peasant's hut you came from." He only granted her one mercy – that she could take with her whatever was dearest to her as a farewell gift.

The queen replied with downcast eyes, "Of course, my husband, if that is your will." She threw her arms around him and kissed him and begged him to drink one last drink with her.

The king didn't know that his drink contained a strong sleeping potion. No sooner had he drunk it than he was fast asleep.

The queen took a fine white sheet and wrapped the king in it, and carried him out to a carriage. Then she drove to the old hut that belonged to her father and laid the king in her own old bed.

The king slept a whole day and night without waking. When he finally came to, he had no idea where he was or what had happened. He called for his servants, but there were no servants.

At last his wife came to his side. She said, "My husband, you told me I could take from the palace whatever was dearest to me, so I did. I took you, for you are more precious to me than the whole world."

The king's eyes filled with tears. "My dearest wife," he said. "you are as wise as ever. You shall be mine, and I shall be yours." And he took her back to the palace, and never parted from her again.

THE EMPEROR'S NEW CLOTHES

Many years ago there was an emperor who was so mad about fashionable new clothes that he spent all his money on dressing up. He never inspected his army, or went to the theatre, or drove through the countryside, unless he had a new outfit to show off. He had different clothes for every hour of the day, and at any time when you might say of another king, "His Majesty is in the council chamber," you could always say of him, "The emperor's in his dressing room."

The emperor's city was a hive of activity, and there were always strangers coming and going. One day a pair of swindlers turned up, claiming to be weavers. Their cloth, they boasted, was not just of the finest quality and design, but had the virtue of being invisible to anyone who was stupid or not fit to hold his job.

What wonderful cloth! thought the emperor. *If I wore it, I would be able to find out which of my courtiers are unfit for their posts, and also be able to tell the clever ones from the stupid. Yes, I must have a suit made at once!* He handed over a large sum of money to the swindlers, so that they could start work straight away.

So the swindlers set up a loom and pretended to be weaving, though in fact there was nothing at all on their loom. They coolly demanded the finest silks and costliest gold thread, which they stuffed into their own packs, and then carried on working at the empty loom into the night.

I wonder how they're getting on with my cloth, thought the emperor. But there was one thing which made him feel uneasy, and that was that a man who was stupid or unfit for his job would not be able to see the cloth. Not that *he* had anything to fear, but all the same he thought it might be best to send someone else first to see how things were going. Everyone in the city had heard about the special virtue of the cloth, and they were all agog to find out how stupid or incompetent their friends were.

I will send my honest old prime minister to the weavers, thought the emperor. *He'll be the best judge of the cloth, for he's got brains, and he's good at his job.*

So the honest old prime minister went to the room where the two swindlers were working away. *Good Lord!* thought the old man, as he goggled at the empty loom. *I can't see a thing!* But he kept that to himself.

The swindlers begged him to be so good as to come closer and tell them what he thought of the cloth. "Do you like the design?" They pointed to the empty loom, but though the poor old man stared and stared he couldn't see a thing. *Oh dear!* he thought. *Does this mean that I am stupid? I never had an inkling, and no one else must either! Or perhaps I am unfit for my job? Whatever, no one must find out that I cannot see the cloth.*

"Now, do you like it or not?" asked one of the weavers.

"Oh, it's charming, absolutely delightful," said the old prime minister, peering through his spectacles. "What a gorgeous pattern! I shall tell the emperor that I am most pleased with it."

"You're too kind," said the swindlers. And then they described the pattern in detail, and the old prime minister listened carefully so that he could repeat it all to the emperor – which he duly did.

The swindlers now asked for more money, silk and gold thread, in order to finish the cloth. But it all went straight into their own pockets. Not a single thread was put on the loom – they just carried on weaving air.

Before long, the emperor sent a second offical to see how work was progressing, and find out when the clothes would be ready. The same things happened to him as to the prime minister. No matter how hard he looked, he could not see anything on the empty loom.

"It's really beautiful, isn't it?" asked one of the swindlers.

I'm not stupid, thought the official, *so I must be unfit for my job. If people found out, I'd be a laughing stock.* So he too praised the material which he couldn't see, and said how pleased he was with its subtle shades and beautiful design.

"It's quite exquisite," he told the emperor.

The wonderful material was the talk of the town. At last, the emperor decided he must go and see it for himself while it was still on the loom. He took along a number of courtiers, including the two honest officials who had already described the cloth, to see the two swindlers working busily at their empty looms.

"Isn't it *magnifique?*" said the two honest officials. "Just look at the pattern, Your Majesty." And they pointed to the empty loom, sure that everyone else could see the cloth.

What's this? thought the emperor. *I can't see anything! Am I stupid? Or am I unfit to be emperor? This is too awful for words.* "Oh! It's wonderful!" he said. "It is everything I hoped for." And he gave a satisfied nod at the empty loom. He wasn't going to admit he couldn't see a thing.

All the others who were there were in the same boat. They could see nothing, but they all said what the emperor said: "Oh! It's wonderful!" They told him he should have some clothes made from the magnificent material in time to wear them at the great procession that was soon to take place. "Magnificent! Wonderful! Superb!" were the words on everyone's lips. They were all delighted. The emperor gave each of the swindlers a knighthood, with a medal to wear in his buttonhole, and the title "knight of the loom."

The swindlers sat up all night before the procession, with more than sixteen candles burning, so that people could see how hard they were working on the emperor's new clothes. They pretended to take the cloth off the loom, made cuts in the air with huge scissors, and sewed with needles that had no thread, and finally they announced, "Look! The emperor's clothes are ready!"

The emperor came with his courtiers, and the weavers held out their arms as if they were carrying something, and said, "Here are the trousers! Here is the jacket! Here is the cloak!" and so on. "The whole suit is as light as a spider's web. You'll feel as if you've got nothing on; that's the beauty of the cloth."

"Yes indeed!" said all the courtiers; but they couldn't see anything, for there was nothing to see.

"If Your Majesty would graciously take off the clothes you are wearing, we shall think it a privilege to help you into the new ones in front of the great mirror."

So the emperor took off all his clothes, and the swindlers went through the motions of fitting him with his new suit, even pretending to fasten the train around his waist. The emperor turned this way and that, preening in the mirror.

"How elegant Your Majesty looks! What a perfect fit!" everyone exclaimed. "What a triumph!"

Then the master of ceremonies announced, "The canopy which will be carried above Your Majesty in the procession is waiting outside."

"I am ready to go," said the emperor. "See how well my new clothes fit!" And he did a final twirl in front of the mirror, pretending to admire his fine clothes.

The chamberlains, who were to carry the emperor's train, fumbled on the floor looking for it. They didn't dare admit they couldn't see anything, so they pretended to pick the train up, and as they walked they held their hands in the air as if they were carrying it.

So the emperor marched in procession under the beautiful canopy, and all the people lining the streets or standing at their windows exclaimed, "The emperor's new clothes are the best he's ever had! What a perfect fit! And just look at the train!" For no one wanted people to think that he couldn't see anything, and so was a fool, or unfit for his job. Never had the emperor's clothes been such a success.

"But he hasn't got anything on!" said a little child.

"Listen to the little innocent!" said the father.

But the whisper passed through the crowd: "He hasn't got anything on! There's a little child who says he hasn't got anything on!" And at last the people shouted with one voice, "He hasn't got anything on!"

The emperor had the uncomfortable feeling that they were right. But he thought, *I must go through with it now.* So he drew himself up to his full height and walked proudly on, and the chamberlains walked behind him carrying the train that wasn't there.

THE FISHERMAN AND HIS WIFE

There was once a fisherman who lived with his wife in a pigsty by the sea. He went fishing every day; and he fished, and he fished.

One day he was sitting with his rod and line, looking into the clear water. And he sat, and he sat.

His line suddenly sank, down, down to the bottom of the sea, and when he pulled it up he had caught a large flounder. And the flounder said, "Listen. I'm not really a flounder. I'm an enchanted prince. So there's no point in killing me I wouldn't be good to eat. Put me back in the water and let me go."

"There's no need to go on," said the fisherman. "If you can talk, you can go free." And he released the flounder back into the sea, and it swam down to the bottom, leaving a streak of blood behind it. Then the fisherman called it a day, and went home to his wife in the pigsty.

"Have you caught nothing at all today?" she asked.

"No," he said. "I did catch a flounder, but it turned out to be an enchanted prince, so I let it go."

"Didn't you make a wish first?"

"No," he said. "What would I wish for?"

"What about somewhere better to live than this filthy pigsty? You could have wished for a little cottage. Go and catch him again, and wish for a cottage. He couldn't deny us that."

"I'm not sure about that," said the fisherman.

"Well I am," said his wife. "Off you go right this minute and catch that flounder." He didn't really want to go, but he knew better than to disobey his wife, so he went.

When he got there the sea was all green and yellow, and no longer crystal clear. He stood on the shore, and said,

> *Flounder, flounder in the sea,*
> *Come, come,*
> *come to me;*
> *For my wife, good Ilsabil,*
> *Has sent me here,*
> *against my will.*

Then the flounder came swimming to him and said, "What does she want?"

"She says that as I caught you, I should have wished for something. She doesn't want to live in a pigsty anymore. She wants a cottage."

"Go home then," said the flounder. "She has it already."

When the man got home his wife was no longer in the pigsty, but in a little cottage. She was sitting on a bench just inside the door. She took him by the hand, and led him through the porch and into the sitting room and the bedroom and the kitchen and the pantry, all the while exclaiming, "Isn't this better?" Best of all was the yard with hens and ducks, and a little garden full of fruit and vegetables. "Isn't it lovely?" said the wife.

"Yes," said fisherman. "It'll do us nicely. We shall be snug as a bug in a rug."

"We'll see," said the wife, and they went off to bed.

All went well for a couple of weeks, but then the wife began to feel dissatisfied. "This cottage is too poky," she said, "and the yard's just a pocket handkerchief. It would have been just as easy for the flounder to give us a bigger house. I fancy a stone castle. Go and tell the flounder to give us a castle."

"I like the cottage," said the fisherman. "What would we want with a castle?"

"Just go and tell him."

"He's only just given us a cottage. I don't like to harass him."

"Go," said the wife. "He'll be glad to do it."

The man's heart was heavy. He said to himself, *It's not right*, yet he went. When he came to the sea, the water was purple and dark blue, quite murky and thick, but not stirred up. He stood on the shore and said,

> *Flounder, flounder in the sea,*
> *Come, come,*
> > *come to me;*
> *For my wife, good Ilsabil,*
> *Has sent me here,*
> > *against my will.*

"What does she want now?" asked the flounder.

"She wants to live in a big stone castle," said the fisherman, all in a fluster.

"Just go home," said the flounder. "She's standing at the door."

So he set off for home, but it wasn't there anymore. He came to a great stone castle, with a huge stone staircase leading to the door, and at the top of the staircase was his wife. She took him by the hand and led him through the marble hall. Servants flung the doors open, and every room was bright with tapestries. The tables and chairs were made of pure gold. There were crystal chandeliers hanging from the ceilings, and fine rugs on the bedroom floors. It was almost too much to take in.

Behind the castle there was a great courtyard, with stables and carriages, and a flower garden, and rolling parkland with a herd of deer in it. It was everything the heart could desire.

"Isn't it wonderful?" said the wife.

"Yes," said the fisherman. "It's beautiful. We shall be happy here."

"We'll see," said the wife, and they went to bed.

Next morning the wife woke first. Day was breaking, and from her bed she could see the beautiful countryside around her. Her husband was still stretching when she poked him in the ribs and said, "Husband, look out of the window. Do you see all that country? We could be king over that. Go to the flounder and tell him we want to be king."

"Why should we want to be king?" said the husband. "I don't want to be king."

"Well," said the wife, "if you don't want to be king, I do. So go to the flounder. I will be king!"

"I can't tell him that," said the man. "Why do you want to be king? Why?"

"Because," said the wife. "Now get going. I must be king."

The husband went, although he wasn't at all happy about it. *It's not right. It's not right*, he thought.

When he came to the sea, it was as dark as charcoal. The water was choppy, and it smelled vile. He went to the shore, and said,

Flounder, flounder in the sea,
Come, come,
    come to me;
For my wife, good Ilsabil,
Has sent me here,
        against my will.

"What does she want now?" said the flounder. "
"She wants to be king."
"The crown is already on her head."
The man went home, and when he got there the castle had become a huge palace with a tower and carvings. There were soldiers with drums and trumpets, and a sentry at the gate. When he went inside, everything was made of marble and gold, with velvet covers and great golden tassels.
The doors of the great hall were open wide, and his wife was holding court from a high throne of gold and diamonds, with a big gold crown on her head. Ladies-in-waiting stood in rows on both sides of her, each a head shorter than the last.
He went and stood before her, and said, "So, wife, you are king."
"Yes," she said. "Now I am king."
Then he stood and looked at her for a while, and after he had finished looking, he said, "Let's leave it there, shall we?"
"No, no," said the wife, quite upset. "Already the time is hanging heavy on

my hands. I can't stand still. Go to the flounder and tell him I want to be emperor."

"I can't say that," said the husband. "How could he make you emperor? There's only one emperor in the empire. He can't do it, I tell you."

"What!" said the wife. "I am the king, and you are nothing but my husband. Don't argue with me – just go at once. If the flounder can make me king, he can make me emperor. Go!"

The man went, but he was very troubled. *Emperor!* he thought. *Emperor is too much. It won't end well. The flounder must be getting sick if this.*

When he came to the sea, it was black and turbid. It was churning up from below, and a sharp wind was whipping it into foam. The man was afraid. But he stood on the shore and said,

> *Flounder, flounder in the sea,*
> *Come, come,*
> > *come to me;*
> *For my wife, good Ilsabil,*
> *Has sent me here,*
> > *against my will.*

"What's she after now?" said the flounder."

"I'm sorry, but she wants to be emperor."

"Go to her," said the flounder, "she is emperor already."

So he went home, and this time the whole palace was made of polished marble, with golden statues. The soldiers were marching up and down outside, blowing trumpets and beating drums, and inside, barons, counts and dukes were acting as servants. They opened the doors for him, and the doors were of pure gold. He found his wife on a throne made out of one block of gold, and it was at least two miles high. She was wearing a great golden crown set with precious stones, and clutching the imperial orb. On either side of her stood a row of guards, each one shorter than the one next to him, from the biggest giant, who was two miles high, to the smallest dwarf, who was no bigger than a finger. Dukes and princes were crowding around her.

The fisherman went and stood alongside them, and said, "So you're emperor now."

"Yes," she said, "I'm emperor."

"Well, you can't go higher than that."

"Oh yes I can," she said. "Now that I'm emperor, I want to be pope too."

"I can't ask the flounder that!" said the husband in alarm. "No, no, you can't be pope. There's only one pope."

"Fiddle-faddle!" she said. "I'm the emperor, and you're only my husband. Go at once to the flounder and tell him I want to be pope."

He felt quite weak in the knees, but he went. He shivered. A cold wind was blowing, and the clouds were flying. It grew dark, and the gusts of wind tore the leaves from the trees. The water roared and foamed as if it were boiling, and the waves crashed against the shore. Out at sea, boats were firing distress flares. There was still a patch of blue in the sky, but mostly it was the fierce red of an angry storm. He stood on the shore in fear and despair, and said,

> *Flounder, flounder in the sea,*
> *Come, come,*
> > *come to me;*
> *For my wife, good Ilsabil,*

Has sent me here,
against my will.

"Well, what does she want?" said the flounder.

"I'm afraid she wants to be pope."

"Go home," said the flounder. "She is pope already."

When he got home, it was a huge cathedral surrounded by palaces. He pushed his way through the crowd. Inside, everything was lit by candles. His wife was dressed in gold, and was sitting on an even higher throne, with three golden crowns. Emperors and kings were on their knees before her, kissing her shoe.

"So," said the fisherman, "now you are pope."

"Yes," she said, "I am pope."

He stood and looked at her, and it was as if he were staring at the sun. When he had finished looking, he said, "I hope you'll be satisfied now. You can't do better than pope."

"We'll see," she said, and they went to bed.

But she couldn't sleep. She was restless and fretful. She couldn't stop thinking what else there was that she could be. All night she tossed and turned, but she couldn't come up with anything.

At sunrise, she saw the red glow of dawn through the window. And when she saw the sun rising, she thought, *Why can't I make the sun and moon rise?*

"Husband!" she shouted, poking him in the ribs with her elbows, "Wake up! Go and see the flounder. I want to be God."

The fisherman was still half asleep, but her words gave him such a jolt that he fell out of bed. He thought he must have misheard. He rubbed his eyes, and said, "What's that?"

"If I can't make the sun and moon rise, I won't be able to bear it. I'll never have another moment's happiness if I can't make them rise." She shot him a look so mad it sent a shiver right through him. "Go at once. I want to be God."

The man flung himself to his knees. "Wife, the flounder can't do that. He can make an emperor and a pope. Please, I beg you, be content with pope."

She fell into a rage. Her hair stood on end, and she began to kick and scream. "I can't stand it," she cried. "I can't stand it for a moment longer. Go!"

He pulled on his trousers and ran wildly out. A storm was raging. The wind was blowing so hard that he could scarcely keep his feet. Trees and houses were falling, and even the mountains were trembling, sending great rocks crashing down into the sea. The sky was pitch black, but in the lightning flashes he could see black waves as big as mountains and as high as church towers, each with a crest of white foam. He couldn't hear his own voice, but he bellowed,

> *Flounder, flounder in the sea,*
> *Come, come,*
> *come to me;*
> *For my wife, good Ilsabil,*
> *Has sent me here,*
> *against my will.*

"What can she want now?" said the flounder.

"She wants to be God," stammered the fisherman.

"Go home," said the flounder. "She's back in the pigsty."
And they are still living there to this day.

THE STEADFAST TIN SOLDIER

O nce there were twenty-five soldiers, all brothers, because they were all made out of the same old tin spoon. They stood up straight with their muskets on their shoulders, very proud in their red and blue uniforms. The very first thing they heard in the world, when the lid of their box was taken off, was "Tin soldiers!" It was a little boy who shouted it, with a clap of his hands. They were a birthday present, and he paraded them on the table.

All the soldiers were exactly alike, except one. He'd only got one leg, because he was made last, and the tin had run out. But he stood just as firm on his one leg as the others did on two, and he's the one this story is about.

There were plenty of other toys on the table where the tin soldiers were set out, but the one that really caught your eye was a paper castle. You could see through its little windows right into the rooms. Outside, tiny trees stood beside a little mirror, which was meant to be a lake. Wax swans swam on it, admiring their own reflections.

It was a lovely scene – and loveliest of all was the girl who stood in the castle's open door. She too was cut out of paper, but her skirt was made of finest muslin, and as a shawl around her shoulders she wore a narrow sky-blue ribbon, fastened with a gleaming star the size of her face. She stretched out her arms, for she was a dancer, and kicked one leg so high that the tin soldier couldn't see it, and thought she'd only got one leg, like him.

"That's just the wife for me," he thought. "But she's so grand. She lives in a castle. I have only a box, and there are twenty-five of us in that. There's no room for her. Still, I'll try to get to know her." So he hid behind a snuff box that was on the table, where he had a good view of the charming dancer, poised with such perfect balance on one leg.

When night came, the other tin soldiers were put back in their box, and the children went to bed. Now it was time for the toys to play. They paid each other visits, waged wars and even held a ball. How the tin soldiers rattled in their box, trying to join in! But they couldn't get the lid off. The nutcracker turned somersaults, and the slate pencil kept score on the slate. They made such a row they woke the canary, and it started speechifying – in verse, too!

Only two never moved. The little dancer stayed on tiptoe with her arms outstretched, and the tin soldier stood steadfast on his single leg, and his eyes never left her for a moment.

And then the clock struck twelve, and *crash*! up jumped the lid of the snuff box. There wasn't any snuff inside, oh no. Out sprang a little black goblin. It was a Jack-in-the-box.

"Tin soldier!" said the goblin. "You keep your eyes to yourself." But the tin soldier pretended not to hear.

"All right," said the goblin. "Just you wait till tomorrow."

And whether it was the goblin's doing or just the wind, no one can say, but next morning, when the children got up, and the little boy put the tin soldier on the windowsill, the window flew open and the tin soldier fell, head over heels, from three floors up. It was a fearful drop. He landed on his head with his leg in the air and his bayonet trapped between two cobblestones.

The maid and the little boy went to look for him there and then, but even though they nearly trod on him they didn't see him. If only he had called out, "Here I am!" they would have found him, but he didn't think it right to make a commotion when he was wearing his uniform.

Now it began to rain, heavier and heavier till it was a real storm. And when it was over, along came two street kids.

"Look!" said one. "Here's a tin soldier! Let's sail him."

So they made a boat out of newspaper and put the tin soldier in it, and away he sailed down the gutter, with the boys running by his side clapping their hands. Heavens above! What waves, what tides there were in that gutter. It had been a real downpour.

The boat plunged up and down and whirled round and round till the tin soldier was quite dizzy. But he stood fast. He never flinched, but looked straight ahead with his musket on his shoulder.

Suddenly the boat ducked into a gutter pipe. It was as dark in there as in his box at home.

"Where am I going now?" he wondered. "Oh, it's all that goblin's fault. But if only the little dancer was by my side, I wouldn't care if it was twice as dark."

Just then a huge rat, who lived in the pipe, darted out. "Passport!" said the rat. "Where's your passport?"

The tin soldier kept quiet and gripped his musket. The boat sailed on and the rat gave chase. Ugh! How he gnashed his teeth, screeching to floating bits of straw and wood, "Stop him! Stop him! He's not paid the toll! He hasn't shown his passport!"

But the current swept faster and faster. The tin soldier could already spy daylight at the end of the pipe, but he could also hear a terrible roaring fit to frighten the bravest of men. Think of it: at the end of the pipe, the water

gushed out into a great canal. It was as risky for him as it would be for us to plunge down a mighty waterfall.

He was so near there was no stopping. The boat raced out, and the poor tin soldier braced himself as stiffly as he could; no one could say he so much as blinked.

The boat spun round three or four times and filled with water to the brim. It had to sink. The tin soldier was in the water up to his neck. Down, down sank the boat. The paper turned to mush, and the water closed over the tin soldier's head. He thought of the lovely little dancer whom he would never see again, and the words of an old song rang in his ears:

> *March on, march on to victory –*
> *Tomorrow you must die.*

The boat fell to bits, the soldier fell through – and at that very moment was swallowed up by a great fish.

Oh my! How dark it was in there! It was even worse than the gutter pipe, and a tighter fit, too. But the tin soldier was steadfast. He lay there, flat out, with his musket over his shoulder. Round and about swam the fish, with all sorts of twists and turns. Then it was still. Then, a bolt of lightning seemed to flash through it. It was the clear light of day, and someone was exclaiming, "A tin soldier!" For the fish had been caught, and taken to market, and sold, and now it was in the kitchen where the cook had cut it open with a big knife.

She picked up the tin soldier round the waist, and carried him between her finger and thumb into the living room. Everyone wanted to see the remarkable character who had voyaged inside a fish. But the tin soldier didn't let it go to his head.

They stood him on the table and – the world is full of wonders – there he was, back in the very room he'd set out from.

Here were the same children, the same toys on the table, the beautiful castle, the graceful little dancer. Still she balanced on just one leg, with the other held high in the air. She, too, was steadfast. The tin soldier was touched to the quick. He could have wept tin tears, if he hadn't been a soldier. He looked at her, and she looked at him, but they never said a word.

Suddenly, the little boy took the soldier and flung him into the stove. Why, he couldn't say. No doubt the goblin in the snuff box was at the bottom of it.

The tin soldier stood in a blaze of light. Whether he burned from the heat of the fire or the heat of his love he did not know. All his paint was gone; whether from the hardships of his journey or the bitterness of his grief, no one could tell.

He looked at the little dancer and she looked at him. He felt himself melting away, but he was steadfast, with his musket on his shoulder. Then the door opened, a draught caught the dancer, and she flew into the stove to the tin soldier. She flared and was gone. And then the tin soldier melted back into a lump of tin.

Next morning, when she raked out the ashes, the maid found him, shaped like a little tin heart. Of the dancer nothing remained, save the star from her breast, and that was burned as black as coal.

THE
MUSICIANS
OF BREMEN

A man had a donkey that served him faithfully for many a long year, hauling sacks of grain to the mill. But at last the donkey's strength began to fail; the work was getting too much for him.

Then the master began to complain about the cost of the donkey's keep, and the donkey, seeing which way the wind was blowing, ran away along the road to Bremen, thinking he might be able to join the town band.

When he had gone some little way he found a dog lying by the road, panting as if he had just run a race.

"Hey-up, shaggy," said the donkey. "What's your problem?"

"Because I am old and can no longer hunt, my master decided to have me put down, so I ran away. But I am weak, so how am I to earn a living?"

"Come with me to Bremen to join the band," said the donkey. "I'll play the lute, and you'll play the drum." The dog perked up at that idea, and the two went along together.

It wasn't long before they saw a cat sitting by the road with a face like a wet week.

"Hey-up, whiskers," said the donkey. "Why so sad?"

"Who can be happy when their life is threatened?" replied the cat. "Just because I am getting old, and my teeth are worn down, my mistress wanted to drown me; so I ran away. But what am I to do now? At my age, I should be sitting by the fire, not out hunting for my supper."

"Come to Bremen with us. You're a born singer, so you can join the band with us." The cat liked the idea, so she went along.

Soon the three runaways came to a farmyard. The rooster was sitting on the gate, crowing at the top of his voice.

"Oh, that sound!" said the donkey. "It sets your teeth on edge. Why are you making such a racket?"

"I'm foretelling good weather, for it's the day Our Lady washes the Christ Child's shirts, so it's bound to be fine drying weather. But it's not so good for me, for tomorrow's Sunday, and we have guests, and I heard the farmer's wife tell the cook to wring my neck tonight and serve me up as soup tomorrow. She has no pity. That's why I'm crowing now, while I still can."

"Red-comb, don't be a fool. Come with us to Bremen. Whatever happens, it's bound to be better than death. You've got a strong voice; maybe if we all sing together we'll really make music!"

The rooster agreed, and the four went on together down the road to Bremen. They could not reach the city before nightfall, so they spent that night in the forest. The donkey and the dog settled down under a big tree, the cat climbed up on a branch and the rooster flew to the top of the tree, where he felt safest. Before going to sleep, he looked around in every direction. He thought he saw a spark in the distance and told his companions that there must be a house nearby, for he had seen a light.

"In that case," said the donkey, "let's go there, for I can't get comfortable under this tree."

The dog agreed. "Where there's a house, there are usually bones," he said, "and bones aren't bad.".

So they set off in the direction of the light. It grew brighter and brighter, until at last they came to a house. It was the house of a gang of robbers.

The donkey, who was the tallest, went to the lit window and peered in. "What can yau see, long-ears?" asked the rooster.

"What can I see?" replied the donkey. "I can see a table covered with good things to eat and drink, and a gang af robbers sitting down and feasting at it."

"That's what we want," said the rooster.

"Oh, ycs! If only!" said the donkey.

But how were they to drive the robbers away? The animals talked it over, and at last they came up with a plan.

The donkey stood with his forefeet on the window ledge. The dog jumped on the donkey's back. The cat climbed on top of the dog. The rooster flew up and landed on the cat's head.

Then they struck up the band. The donkey brayed, the dog barked, the cat meowed and the rooster crowed. Then they leaped through the window and landed in the room in a shower of glass.

The robbers thought it must be a monster. They were so frightened that they fled into the forest, leaving the house for the animals, who settled themselves at the table and ate their fill.

When the four musicians could eat no more, they put out the light and found themselves places to sleep. The donkey lay down on the dung heap in the yard. The dog lay by the back door. The cat curled up on the warm ashes in the hearth. And the rooster perched up on top of the roof. Being tired out from their long walk, they soon went to sleep.

When it was past midnight, the robbers saw from a distance that the light had gone out. They began to think they had been fools to be scared off so easily. The chief robber told one of the others to go and have a look-see.

The robber crept in through the front door. All was quiet, but it was too dark to see. He went to the fire to try to light a match. The cat opened her eyes, and the robber, thinking they were burning embers, held the match up to them.

The cat didn't think this was funny. She sprang at the robber's face, spitting and scratching.

Scared to bits, the robber ran to the back door, but the dog jumped up and bit him in the leg.

The robber stumbled out into the yard, but as he passed the dung heap the donkey kicked him with his strong hind legs.

The rooster, who had been woken by all the commotion, started crowing from the roof, "What-a-to-do! What-a-to-do!"

At that the robber ran back as fast as he could to his fellows and said, "There's a horrible witch in the house, who spat at me and scratched my face with her long claws. Behind the door, there's a man with a knife, who stabbed me in the leg. In the yard, there's a huge monster who hit me on the head with a wooden club. And above them all, sitting on the roof, is a judge, who called out, 'The jailhouse for you! The jailhouse for you!' I only just made it out by the skin of my teeth."

The robbers never dared go near the house again, and as the four musicians liked it so well, they never left it. And the mouth of the last person who told this story is still warm.

RUMPELSTILTSKIN

Once there was a miller who was very poor but had a beautiful daughter. One day he happened to be talking to the king and, to puff himself up, he said, "My daughter can spin straw into gold."

The king said to the miller, "How fascinating! If your daughter is as clever as you say, bring her to the palace tomorrow, and we'll see what she can do."

When the girl was brought to him he took her into a room full of straw, gave her a spinning wheel, and said, "Off you go then! I'm sure you'll have spun all this straw into gold by tomorrow morning. But if you haven't, you must die."

He locked her in the room and left her there alone.

The poor girl sat there, and for the life of her she didn't know what to do. She hadn't the first idea how to spin straw into gold. She was so terrified she began to cry.

All at once the door opened, and in stepped a little man. "Good evening," he said. "Why are you crying so?"

"Oh," she said, "I'm supposed to spin straw into gold, and I don't know how."

"What will you give me if I spin it for you?"

"My necklace," said the girl.

The little man took the necklace, sat down at the wheel, and *whirr, whirr, whirr*, three turns, and the reel was full. Then he put on another, and *whirr, whirr, whirr*, three turns, and the second reel was full. All night he worked, and in the morning all the straw was spun and all the reels were full of gold.

The king came first thing in the morning, and when he saw the reels of gold he was delighted. His heart swelled with greed. He took the miller's daughter to a larger room full of straw and told her to spin this too into gold if she valued her life.

She didn't know what to do, and she was crying, when the door opened, and the little man appeared. He said, "What will you give me if I spin this straw into gold for you?"

"The ring from my finger."

The little man took the ring, sat down at the wheel, and by morning he had spun all the straw into glittering gold.

The king was full of joy at the sight; but still he didn't have enough gold. He took the girl to a still larger room full of straw and said, "You must spin this into gold tonight. If you succeed, you shall be my wife." He said to himself, *She may only be a miller's daughter, but I couldn't find a richer wife in the whole world.*

When the girl was alone, the little man came in for the third time, and said, "What will you give me if I spin the straw into gold for you this time?"

"I have nothing left to give," said the girl.

"Then promise me, if you should ever become queen, to give me your first child."

Who knows what life will bring? thought the girl. She had no choice but to promise the little man what he wanted, and for that he spun the straw into gold.

When the king came in the morning and found all as he wished, he married her, and the miller's pretty daughter became a queen.

A year later, she brought a beautiful baby into the world. She had forgotten all about the little man. But suddenly he came into her room, and said, "Now give me what you promised."

The queen was horror-struck. She offered him all the riches in the kingdom if he would let her keep the child. But the little man said, "A living soul is more precious to me than all the treasures in the world."

The queen wept so bitterly that the little man took pity on her. "I will give you three days' grace. If, in that time, you can find out my name, you may keep the child."

The queen tossed and turned all night, thinking of every name she had ever heard of, and she sent a messenger across the country to ask what other names there might be. When the little man came next day, she began with Caspar, Melchior and Balthazar, and reeled off every name she knew, one after another; but to everyone the little man said, "That is not my name."

On the second day she sent the messenger back out to ask for names, and she tried all the unusual ones on the little man.

"Is your name Sparerib, or Sheepshank, or Laceleg?"
But he always answered no.

On the third day the messenger told her, "As I walked at the edge of the forest, where the fox and the hare bid each other good night, I came to the foot of a mountain. There I saw a little hut, and outside the hut a fire was blazing. A funny little man was hopping around the fire, singing,

> *Today I brew, tomorrow bake,*
> *And after that the child I'll take.*
> *I'm the winner of the game,*
> *Rumpelstiltskin is my name."*

The queen was so glad to hear that!

Soon the little man arrived. He said, "Now, Your Majesty, what is my name?"

"Is it Tom?"

"No."

"Is it Dick?"

"No."

"Is it Harry?"

"No"

"Could it be . . . Rumpelstiltskin?"

"The devil told you that," the little man screamed. "The devil told you that!" He was so angry that he stamped his right foot so deep into the ground that his whole leg went in. Then in his rage he pulled his left foot so hard that he tore himself in two.

So the queen kept her baby, and loved it all the more because she had so nearly lost it.

MANYFURS

There was once a king who had a wife with golden hair. She was so beautiful that there was none on earth to compare with her. When she fell ill and knew that she must soon die, she called the king to her and said, "If you wish to marry again after my death, promise me that you won't take anyone who isn't as beautiful as me and who hasn't got golden hair like mine." And after the king had given his word, she closed her eyes and died.

For a long time the king grieved and had no thought of marrying again. But at last his councillors told him, "You must re-marry." For the king had no son, but only a daughter.

Messengers were sent far and wide looking for a bride who was as beautiful as the late queen and who had such golden hair, but there was no one. So the messengers came home empty handed.

The only person who was as beautiful as the queen and who had such lovely golden hair was the king's own daughter. And one day the king, who was really half out of his mind with grief and worry, said, "I shall marry my daughter."

The councillors told him that he must not. "God forbids it," they said. "No good would come from such a sin. You will drag the whole kingdom down to hell with you."

But the king was determined. "She is the only one who looks like my dear wife, so she is the one I should marry," he said.

The daughter was even more shocked when she heard of the plan, and decided she must hinder it. So she told him, "Before I consent to marry you, I must have three dresses, one as golden as the sun, one as silver as the moon, and one as bright and sparkling as the stars. Also, I must have a cloak made from a thousand different furs, and one of every kind of animal in the kingdom must give a piece of its skin for it." For she thought that the king would never be able to find such garments.

But the king set all the seamstresses and all the hunters in the kingdom to work, and at length all the garments were ready: three dresses, as golden as the stars, as silver as the moon, and as bright as the stars and a cloak made of a thousand different furs.

As the king spread out the many-furred cloak he said, "Tomorrow shall be our wedding day."

When the princess saw that there was no hope of changing the king's mind, she resolved to run away. That night when everyone was asleep, she got up, and took three things from among her treasures – a golden ring, a tiny golden spinning wheel and a tiny golden bobbin. Then she put her dresses of the sun, moon and stars into a nutshell, put on her cloak of a thousand furs, rubbed dirt into her face and hands, and walked out into the forest, trusting to God to watch over her. She walked until she was exhausted, and then she curled up asleep in a hollow log.

The sun rose, but she went on sleeping. She was still asleep when the sun was high. Now it so happened that the king to whom this forest belonged was hunting in it. When his dogs came to the tree, they sniffed, and ran around the tree, barking. The king ordered his huntsman to see what wild beast was hiding there.

"It's a strange beast," the huntsman reported. "I've never seen its like. It is lying asleep in a hollow log, and its skin is covered with a thousand different furs."

The king said, "Try and catch it alive. Tie it to the wagon and take it home."

When the huntsman grabbed hold of the princess, she awoke with a start, and cried in terror, "Have pity on me! I'm a poor child, abandoned by my father and mother. Look after me."

He said, "Manyfurs, you can come and work in the kitchen. You can sweep up the ashes." And she was bundled into the wagon and taken back to the palace. She was given a hidey-hole under the stairs to sleep in, where the sun never shone, and told, "This is your place, Manyfurs." Then she was sent into the kitchen to do the heavy work. They made her carry wood and water, sweep the hearth, pluck the chickens, clean the vegetables, rake the ashes – all the dirty jobs.

Manyfurs lived a wretched life. Alas, fair princess, what's to become of you?

After a long time, a ball was given in the palace, and she asked the chef, "May I go upstairs and watch for a little while? I'll stay outside the door."

The chef said, "Yes, but you must be back in half an hour to sweep the hearth."

Manyfurs took her oil lamp into her hidey-hole, took off her cloak of a thousand furs, washed the grime off her face and hands, and let her beauty shine once more. Then she opened the nutshell and took out her dress as golden as the sun.

As she made her way up to the ballroom, everyone made way for her. No one recognized her. They thought she must be a princess. The king himself came up to her, took her hand, and danced with her. He thought in his heart,

This is the most beautiful girl in the world.

When the dance ended, she curtsied. The king looked away for a moment, and when he looked back, she was gone. No one had seen her leave. The king had all the guards questioned, but no one knew where she had come from or where she had gone.

She had run into her hidey-hole, slipped out of her dress, rubbed dirt on her face and hands, put on her cloak of a thousand furs, and become Manyfurs again.

She went to the kitchen to sweep the hearth, but the chef said, "Never mind with that now. I want to see the dancing, so you make some soup for the king, and mind you don't drop any hairs in it or you'll get no supper."

The chef went upstairs, and Manyfurs made bread soup for the king as best she knew how. Then she fetched her golden ring from her hidey-hole and put it in the bowl.

When the ball was over, the king ate the soup, and he liked it very much. When he got to the bottom of the bowl, he found the golden ring and wondered how it had got there. So he sent for the chef.

The chef was terrified. "You must have let a hair fall into the soup," he said, "and if you have, you shall be beaten for it."

When he came before the king, the king asked him who made the soup.

"I did," he replied.

"That is not true," said the king. "Tonight's soup was different. It was much better than usual."

So the chef had to admit that it was Manyfurs who made the soup.

"Then send her to me," said the king.

When Manyfurs came, the king said, "Who are you?"

"I'm a poor girl abandoned by her father and mother," she replied.

"What's your position here?"

"I'm here for people to throw boots at."

The king produced the ring. "Where did this ring come from ?"

"What would poor Manyfurs know about a ring like that?" she replied. So the king got nothing out of her and had to send her back to the kitchen.

After a while, the king threw another ball. As before, Manyfurs begged the chef for leave to look on. "Yes," he answered, "but be sure to be back in half an hour to make the king that bread soup he likes so much." She nipped into her hidey-hole, threw off her cloak, washed, and opened the nutshell to take out the dress as silver as the moon.

She looked as lovely as could be. The king danced with her, but once more she managed to slip away without being noticed.

She turned herself into Manyfurs again and made the king his soup. This time she slipped her tiny golden spinning wheel into the bowl.

Once again, the king summoned the chef and asked who had made the soup, and once again he admitted, "Manyfurs." But the king could get nothing more out of her this time, just that her place was to have boots thrown at her and what would she know of a golden spinning wheel?

The king held a third ball, and it was just the same as before. Manyfurs begged to go and watch, and the chef let her, saying, "Be sure and come back in time to make the king's soup. I think you must be a witch, Manyfurs, and put a spell on your soup to make the king like it so much better than mine."

She put on the dress that glittered like the stars and went into the ballroom. Once more, the king danced with the beautiful girl and thought that she had never looked so radiant. And while they were dancing he managed, without her noticing, to slip the golden ring onto her finger.

Every time the music seemed to be stopping, the king signalled to the musicians to keep going. But at last it came to an end, and though the king tried to hold on to her, the girl tore herself loose and sprang away so quickly that she vanished before his eyes.

She rushed to her hidey-hole. She didn't have time to take off her dress of stars, but just threw her fur cloak on top of it. And when she rubbed the dirt onto her face and hands, she missed the finger with the ring.

Then she went back to the kitchen as Manyfurs and cooked the king's soup. This time, she hid the tiny golden bobbin at the bottom of the bowl.

When the king found the bobbin, he sent for Manyfurs. Noticing her white finger with the ring on it, he grasped her by the hand and held her fast. When she tried to struggle free, her cloak slipped aside, revealing the dress as bright and sparkling as the stars. The king pulled the many-furred cloak aside, and her lovely hair came tumbling down in a shower of gold. She could conceal herself beneath her many-furred cloak no longer. She washed the dirt from her face and hands and stood there in her glory, more beautiful than anyone who has ever been seen on earth.

The king said, "You are my dear bride, and we shall never part." They were married that day, and they lived happily ever after.

MOTHER SNOW

There was a widow who had two daughters. One of them was pretty and hardworking, while the other was ugly and lazy. But she was much fonder of the ugly, lazy one, because she was her own daughter, so she made her pretty stepdaughter do all the hard work of the house. Every day the poor girl had to sit by a well on the roadside and spin until her fingers bled.

Now it happened that one day when she bled on the spindle she dipped it in the well to wash it clean. But she lost her grip, and the spindle fell to the bottom. She burst into tears and ran to tell her stepmother what had happened. The stepmother gave her a tongue-lashing, and said, "You dropped it, so you must fetch it back."

So the girl went back to the well. She was at her wits' end, and, not knowing what else to do, she cast herself into the well in pursuit of the spindle. She lost her senses, and when she came to she was in a delightful meadow. The sun was shining, and the meadow was starred with lovely flowers.

She crossed the meadow, and after a while she came to a baker's oven full of bread. The bread cried out,

Take me out,
I'm done to a turn.
Take me out
Before I burn!

So she picked up the bread shovel and took out the loaves one by one.

She went on and came to a tree groaning with apples, and it cried out,

Pick me now,
My apples are ripe.
Shake me, shake me
With all your might!

So she shook the tree, and the apples fell like rain. When there were none left on the tree, she piled them up, and went on her way.

Finally she came to a little house. An old woman was peering out of the window, and she had such big teeth that the girl was frightened and almost ran away. But the old woman called out to her, "There's nothing to be scared of. Stay with me and do my housework. If you serve me well, you won't regret it. Just take care to make my bed well, and shake it till the feathers fly – for then it will snow on earth. I am Mother Snow."

As the old woman spoke so kindly, the girl took heart and agreed to stay with her. She did her work well and always shook the bed so hard that the feathers flew about like snowflakes. It was a pleasant life. The old woman never scolded her, and there were roasts or stews to eat every day.

Nevertheless, after a time the girl grew sad. At first she didn't know what was wrong, but then she realized she was homesick. Even though she was a thousand times better off here than at home, still she longed to go back. At last she said to the old woman, "I'm homesick. Although it's so nice here, I can't stay. I must go home."

Mother Snow said, "I'm glad you love your home. As you've served me so well, I shall take you there myself." Then she took the girl by the hand and led her to a doorway. The door was open, and as the girl went through a shower of gold fell on her, and covered her from head to toe. "That's your reward for your service," said Mother Snow. And then she gave the girl back the spindle she had dropped down the well.

When the door closed behind her, the girl was back on the earth again, not far from home. As she entered the yard, the rooster that was sitting on the well crowed,

Cock-a-doodle-doodle-doo!
Our golden girl's come home –
It's true!

Then she went inside, and because she was covered in gold, her stepmother and sister made her welcome.

She told them everything that had happened, and when the mother heard how she had come by such wealth, she thought that the ugly, lazy daughter deserved the same. So she told her to sit by the well and spin until her fingers bled. But the girl just stuck her hand in a thorn bush to prick it, threw the spindle in the well and jumped in after it.

She woke in the same beautiful meadow as her sister, and took the same path across it. When she came to the bread oven, the bread cried out,

Take me out,
I'm done to a turn.
Take me out
Before I burn!

But the lazy girl answered, "Why should I get all dirty for you?" and walked on.

Soon she came to the apple tree, which cried,

Pick me now,
My apples are ripe.
Shake me, shake me
With all your might.

But she answered, "Shake yourself! An apple might fall on my head," and walked on.

When she arrived at Mother Snow's house she wasn't afraid, for she had been warned about the big teeth, so she agreed right away to work for her.

The first day she made the effort to work hard and do everything Mother Snow asked of her; the thought of all that money kept her going. But the second day she eased up, and the third day she barely lifted a finger, and after that she didn't bother to get up at all. She didn't even make Mother Snow's bed properly, and didn't shake it till the feathers flew.

Soon Mother Snow had had enough of her slovenly ways, and sent her packing. The girl was glad enough to go, for she was eager to get her share of gold. Mother Snow led her to the doorway, but as she passed through, a cauldron of sticky tar emptied itself over her. "That's your reward for your service," said Mother Snow, and shut the door.

So the lazy girl went home, all dripping with tar. When the rooster on the rim of the well saw her he crowed,

> *Cock-a-doodle-doodle-doo!*
> *Our dirty girl's come home –*
> *It's true!*

And the tar wouldn't come off. It stuck to her as long as she lived.

THE
BEETLE

The emperor's horse was given gold shoes – a gold shoe for each hoof.
Why was he given gold shoes?

He was a handsome beast – good legs, wise eyes and a mane that fell over his neck like a silken veil. He had borne his master through bullets and smoke on the battlefield – he had used his teeth and hooves to clear a way through the enemy and had jumped right over a fallen horse to carry the emperor to safety. He had saved the emperor's golden crown, and his life as well – and that was even more precious than gold. So that was why he was given gold shoes – a gold shoe for each hoof.

Then the dung beetle came out of the manure heap.

"First the big, then the little," he said, holding out a foot to the blacksmith. "Not that size is important."

"What do you want?" asked the smith.

"Gold shoes," replied the beetle.

"Are you mad?" said the smith. "Why should you get gold shoes?"

"Why not?" said the beetle. "Aren't I as good as that clumsy brute, who needs to be waited on hand and foot – groomed, fed and watered? Don't I live in the same stable?"

"But why has the horse been given its gold shoes? You don't understand!"

"Understand! I understand when I'm not wanted!" said the beetle. "Insults and ridicule! I've had enough. I'm going out into the world to make my fortune."

"Good riddance to bad rubbish," said the smith.

"Oaf!" said the beetle.

Then the beetle flew outside, to a flower garden filled with the scent of roses and lavender.

"Isn't it lovely here?" asked a ladybug, showing off the smart black spots on her red wings. "Isn't it fragrant?"

"It's not a patch on what I'm used to," said the beetle. "Call this beautiful? Why, there isn't even a manure heap."

The beetle flew over to the shade of a gillyflower, on which a furry caterpillar was crawling. "What a wonderful world this is!" said the caterpillar. "The sun is so warm; everything is perfect. And when I fall asleep – what some people call dying – I shall wake up as a butterfly."

"Wherever did you get such a notion?" said the beetle. "Don't give yourself airs! I come from the emperor's stable, and no one there not even the emperor's horse – has ideas like that. Go on, grow some wings and flyaway! I'm going to." And the beetle flew off.

"I try not to get annoyed," he muttered, "but I am annoyed, all the same." So he dropped onto the lawn, and went to sleep.

Then the heavens opened – it poured with rain. The beetle was woken up by the rain, and he tried to burrow into the earth, but he couldn't. The water overturned him – now he was swimming on his front, now his back. Flying was out of the question. It looked like this would be the end for him. There was nothing to do but lie there – so there he lay.

When the rain stopped for a moment and the beetle blinked the water out of his eyes, he caught sight of something white. It was a piece of linen left out on the grass to dry. It was soaking wet. The beetle crept into a fold. It wasn't as good as the manure heap, but beggars can't be choosers. So he stayed there for a day and a night, and the rain stayed too. The beetle didn't poke his head out of the fold until morning; he was that vexed.

Two frogs came and plopped down on the linen. Their eyes were shining with pleasure. "What glorious weather!" one said. "It's so refreshing, and this linen really soaks it up! You could swim in it!"

The other said, "I'd like to know if the swallow, who can't stay in one place for five minutes, has ever come across a better climate than ours. Such drizzle and damp! It's as good as living in a ditch. A frog who is tired of such weather is tired of life."

"I don't suppose you've ever been in the emperor's stables," said the beetle, "but there, the wetness is spicy and warm. That's my kind of damp – but you can't take it with you when you travel. Can you tell me, is there a greenhouse in this garden, where a refined type like me would feel at home?"

The frogs couldn't understand him – or rather they wouldn't.

"I only ask once," said the beetle, after he had asked three times and never got an answer.

He went on and came to a bit of broken flowerpot. It shouldn't have been left lying there; but as it had been, several families of earwigs had taken shelter under it. Earwigs don't need a lot of room; but they do like company. The mothers all love their children and think that they are the cleverest and most beautiful of all.

"My boy is engaged already," said one. "The little innocent! So full of boyish pranks! His ambition is to climb into a priest's ear. Bless him!"

"My boy," said another, "is a likely lad – he came sizzling out of the egg, and he's sowing his wild oats already. And that warms a mother's heart. Don't you agree, Mr. Beetle?" For she had recognized him by his shape.

"You are both right," said the beetle, so they invited him to come in and make himself at home.

"You must meet my little one," said a third mother.

"They're such sweethearts, and so full of fun," said a fourth. "They're never naughty unless they have a tummy ache – though they do get rather a lot of those."

All the mothers chattered on about their children, and the children themselves pulled at the beetle's beard with the little pincers they have in their tail.

"The little rascals!" said the mothers. "Always up to something!" And they positively dribbled with motherly love. But the beetle was bored, and asked directions to the greenhouse.

"It's far, far away, on the other side of the ditch," said one of the earwig mothers. "If one of my children were to travel so far from home, it would be the death of me."

"All the same that's where I'm going," said the beetle, and he left without saying goodbye, as important people do.

In the ditch he came across some relatives – all dung beetles.

"We live here," they said. "We're as snug as bugs. It's the land of plenty! Come in, you must have had a tiring journey."

"Yes, I have," said the beetle. "I've been lying on linen in the rain, and there's only so much cleanliness a beetle can bear. And now I've got aches and pains in my wings from standing under a draughty piece of flowerpot. What a relief to be back among my own kind!"

"Do you come from the greenhouse?" asked the oldest of them. "Higher up," said the beetle. "I was born with gold shoes on my feet; I come from the emperor's stable. Now I've been sent on a secret mission. But it's no use pumping me about it – I won't say a word."

With that the beetle eased itself down into the mud.

There were three girl beetles there, giggling out of nervousness.

"They're none of them engaged," said their mother, and the girls giggled out of shyness.

"Even in the royal stables, I've never seen more beautiful girls," said the adventurous beetle.

"Don't take advantage of my little girls! Don't pay court to them unless you mean it. But I see you are a gentleman, so I give you my blessing."

"Hurrah!" cried all the others, and so the beetle became engaged. First engaged; then married; there was no reason for delay.

The first day was good enough; the second jogged along; but by the third day it was all too much – he couldn't be doing with wives and maybe even children.

They took me by surprise, thought the beetle. *So now I'll surprise them.*

And he did. He ran away. His wives waited all day and all night, and then they knew they had been abandoned. The other beetles said, "He was a good-for-nothing playboy," because now they would have to take care of his deserted wives.

"So now you are innocent young girls again," said their mother. "But shame on that no-good for leaving you like that!"

In the meantime the beetle was sailing across the ditch on a cabbage leaf. Two men taking a morning stroll happened to see him, and picked him up. They turned him this way and that and looked at him from every angle, for they were experts.

The younger one said, "'Allah sees the black beetle in the black stone in the black mountain.' Isn't that what it says in the Koran?" And then he

translated the beetle's name into Latin and gave an account of its species and their habits. But the older one said, "There's no need to take this one home; we have better specimens already."

The beetle's feelings were hurt by this, so he flew out of the scholar's hand and up into the sky. His wings had dried off, so he made it all the way to the greenhouse. A window was open, so he flew straight in and made himself at home in some fresh manure.

"This is the life!" he said.

Soon he fell asleep and dreamed that the emperor's horse was dead and that he, Mr. Beetle, had been given its gold shoes and promised two more. It was a sweet dream.

When the beetle woke up, he climbed out of the manure and took a look about him. How magnificent the greenhouse was! The sun was shining down through the palm leaves onto flowers as red as fire, as yellow as amber and as white as new-fallen snow.

"Such greenery!" exclaimed the beetle. "It will be delicious once it goes bad. What a fine larder! Now I must see if I can find any of my relations here. I can't mix with just anybody; I have my pride and I'm proud of it." And then he allowed himself to daydream about the emperor's horse dying, and being given its gold shoes.

Suddenly a hand grabbed the beetle, pinching him and turning him over.

It was the gardener's son and one of his friends; they had seen the beetle and wanted to have some fun with him. They wrapped him in a vine leaf and put him in a warm trouser pocket, where he wriggled about until he got another pinch from the gardener's son.

The boys ran down to the lake at the bottom of the garden. They made a boat out of an old wooden clog. A stick was the mast, and the beetle – who was tied to the stick with a thread of wool – was the captain. Then the boat was launched.

The lake was so big the beetle thought it was the ocean. He flipped over on his back from fright and lay there lashed to the mast, with all his legs kicking in the air.

The wooden clog sailed across the water. When it got too far out, one of the boys would roll up his trousers and fetch it back. But then, the boys were wanted. They were called so sharply they ran home and forgot all about the boat. It drifted on and on. The beetle was terrified, but he couldn't fly away, as he was tied to the mast.

A fly buzzed up to him.

"Lovely weather we're having," said the fly. "And what a delightful spot this is. Just the place for a snooze in the sun."

"Stuff and nonsense!" said the beetle. "Can't you see I'm tied up?"

"I'm not tied up," said the fly, and flew away.

"Now I know the world," said the beetle. "It's a mean world, and I'm the only decent one in it. First I'm refused my gold shoes; then I'm made to lie on damp linen and stand in a draught; then I'm tricked into marriage. When I boldly set out into the world to try my luck, up comes some human puppy who ties me up and sets me adrift on the raging waves. And all this while the emperor's horse is prancing around in his gold shoes! That's what really riles me. And do I get any sympathy?

"What a life I've had – but what's the use if no one knows my story? The world doesn't deserve to hear it. Not after refusing me gold shoes when the emperor's horse just had to stretch out its legs for them. No, they had their chance. I would have been a credit to the stable. But it's their loss; the world's loss. It's all over."

But all was not over, for two girls were rowing on the pond. "Look! There's a wooden clog!" said one.

"It's got a beetle tied up in it!" said the other. And she lifted the boat out of the water and carefully cut the thread with a small pair of scissors, without harming the beetle. When they reached the shore, she set him down safely on the grass. "Off you go!" she said. "Crawl small or fly high – go on, try!"

The beetle flew straight in through the open window of a large building – and collapsed into the long silken mane of the emperor's horse, who was standing in the stable where they both belonged. He clung tight to the mane while he tried to gather his thoughts.

Here I am, sitting on the emperor's horse, riding high. . . . What was that! Yes, now it's coming clear. Now I understand. Why was the horse given gold shoes? That's what the smith asked me. And now I know. It's for me. That's why the horse was given gold shoes.

The beetle was happy now. "Travel broadens the mind," he said, "and puts everything into perspective."

The sun shone bright through the window. "It's not such a bad world after all," said the beetle, "if you learn to roll with the punches." All was right with the world now, for the emperor's horse had been given gold shoes so that the dung beetle could ride him.

Now I'll dismount, thought the beetle, *and go and tell the other beetles what has been done for me. I'll tell them all my adventures in the wide world. But I won't go on my travels again. I'll stay at home, until the horse wears out his gold shoes.*

THE
LITTLE
MATCH GIRL

It was bitter cold and snowing hard, and it was almost dark; the last evening of the old year was drawing in. But despite the cold and dark, one poor little girl was still astray in the streets, with nothing on her head and nothing on her feet. She had slippers on when she left home, but they were her mother's and too big for her, and they dropped from her feet when she scampered across the road between two carriages. One slipper just disappeared and the other was snatched away by a little boy who wanted it as a doll's cradle.

So the little girl walked on, and her bare feet turned blue and raw with the cold. In her hand she carried a bundle of matches, and there were more in her ragged apron. No one had bought any matches the livelong day; no one had given her so much as a penny. And so she walked on, shivering and starved, poor girl.

The snowflakes fell on her long blond hair, which curled so prettily on her shoulders. But she was not thinking of her beauty, nor of the cold, for lights were winking from every window and the aroma of roast goose was in the air. It was New Year's Eve, and that was what the girl was thinking of.

She sat down in a sheltered corner and snuggled her feet under her, but it was no use. She couldn't get them warm. She didn't dare go home, for she had sold no matches and not earned so much as a penny. Her father would beat her, and anyway her home was nearly as cold as the street. It was an attic, and despite the straw and rags stuffed into the worst holes in the roof, the wind and snow still whistled through.

Her hands were numb with cold. If only she dared strike a single match, perhaps that would warm them. She took one out and struck it on the wall. Ah! The flame was bright and warm, and she held her hands to it. It burned for her with a magic light, until it seemed as if she were sitting by a great iron stove, with a lovely fire burning in it. The girl stretched out her feet to warm them too, but oh! The flame died down. The stove was gone, and the little girl was frozen and alone, with the burnt match in her hand.

She struck a second match against the wall. It flamed, and wherever its light fell the wall thinned to a veil so that the little girl could see into the room within. She saw a table spread with a snow-white cloth all set with fine china, and a piping hot roast goose stuffed with apples and plums. Best of all, the goose – with the knife and fork still in its breast – jumped down from the dish and waddled along the floor right up to the poor child. Then the match burned out, and the girl was left alone beside the cold, thick wall.

She kindled another match. Now she was sitting under a lovely Christmas tree, far bigger and more beautifully decorated than the one she had peeped at through the glass doors of a rich merchant's house last Christmas. A thousand candles were glimmering in the branches, and little painted figures such as she had seen in shop windows were looking down at her from the tree. The girl reached out her hand towards them, and the match went out. But still the Christmas candles burned higher and higher; she could see them twinkling like stars in the sky. Then one of them fell, leaving a trail of fiery light.

"Now someone is dying," said the little girl, for her grandmother, who was

the only person who had been kind to her, but who was now dead, had told her that when a star falls, a soul is going to God.

She struck another match against the wall. It lit, and there, clear and bright in its glow, stood her old grandmother, as gentle and loving as ever.

"Grandmother!" shouted the little girl. "Take me with you! I know you will leave me when the match goes out. You will vanish like the warm stove, the delicious roast goose and the beautiful big Christmas tree!" Feverishly the little girl struck all the rest of the matches in her bundle, to keep her grandmother there. The matches blazed like radiant bright sunshine. Never had Grandmother looked so beautiful and so tall. She lifted the little girl in her arms, and they flew together in glory and joy, higher and higher, beyond cold, beyond hunger, beyond fear, to God.

They found her in the early morning, sitting in the corner of the wall with rosy cheeks and a smile on her lips, frozen to death on the last night of the old year. The new year's sun rose over the little body, sitting with her bundle of matches all burned out. "She was trying to warm herself," people said. But no one knew what beautiful visions she had seen, nor how gloriously she and her grandmother were seeing in the glad new year.

THE
UGLY DUCKLING

It was the height of summer in the countryside. The corn was yellow; the oats were ripe; the hay was stacked in the green meadows, where the stork wandered on his long red legs, muttering to himself in Egyptian, a language he learned from his mother. The open fields were skirted by thick woods, and hidden in the woods were deep cool lakes. Yes, it was lovely out in the country.

The bright sun fell on an old manor-house, and glinted on the moat that surrounded it. On the wall by the water's edge grew huge dock leaves – the biggest were so tall that a child could make a secret hideaway beneath them. The place was as densely tangled as the heart of the woods, and it was here that a duck was sitting on her nest, waiting for her ducklings to hatch. That's a long job, and she was getting tired of it. No one ever came to visit her; the other ducks swimming around in the moat never thought to drop in under the dock leaves for a quack.

But at last the eggs began to crack, one after another. "*Peep! Peep!*" All the chicks were poking their little heads out of their shells.

"*Quack quack!*" said the mother duck, and the little ones waddled to their feet as best they could, staring all the time at the green world under the dock leaves; she let them look as long as they liked, as green is good for the eyes.

"How big the world is!" said the ducklings; and to be sure, there is more room under a leaf than inside an egg.

"Do you suppose that this is the whole world?" said the mother. "Why, the world stretches far away – right across the garden and into the parson's field, though I've never ventured so far myself. Now, are you all hatched?" And she got up from the nest. "No, not all. The largest egg is still here. How much longer will it be? I'm so tired of this." And she sat down again.

An old duck happened by, and asked how she was getting on.

"There's just one egg that's taking forever to hatch. But look at the others: they're the prettiest ducklings you ever did see. They take after their father – that scapegrace, why does he never come and see me?"

"Let me see that egg," said the old duck. "I bet it's a turkey's egg. I was fooled that way once, and the chicks gave me no end of trouble. They were afraid of the water, if you can believe it, and I just couldn't coax them in. I quacked and clucked but it was no use. Let me see it – yes, that's a turkey's egg. Leave it, and teach the others how to swim."

"I'll sit on it a while longer," replied the mother duck. "I've been at it so long, I may as well finish the job."

"Please yourself," said the old duck, and she waddled away.

At long last the big egg cracked open. "*Peep! Peep!*" said the little one, as he tumbled out. How ugly and overgrown he was! The duck looked at him. "What a huge duckling that is! Can it be a turkey after all? Well, there's only one way to find out. Into the water he shall go, if I have to push him in myself."

The weather next day was glorious, so the mother took all her family down to the moat in the sunshine. Splash! she jumped into the water. "*Quack, quack!*" she called, and one by one the ducklings plopped in. The water closed over their heads, but they all bobbed up again, and began to swim happily on the surface, their little feet paddling away beneath them. They were all there, even the ugly one.

"Well, it's not a turkey," said the duck. "Look at those legs go! He knows how to keep upright – he is my own chick! And really quite pretty, if you look closely. *Quack, quack!* Follow me, and I will show you the world – that is, the farmyard. Stay close to me, and keep your eyes skinned for the cat."

So they went into the farmyard. Two duck families were making a terrible

commotion, squabbling over the head of an eel – and then the cat got it after all.

"That's the way of the world," said the mother, with a down turned beak, for she could have just fancied a bit of eel's head. "Now then, use your legs; slip over and pay your respects to that old duck over there. She is our most distinguished resident; she has Spanish blood. And look, she has a piece of red cloth tied round her leg. That marks her out as special – no one would dream of behaving rudely to her. Look lively, and don't turn your toes in; a well-bred duckling splays its feet out, like its father and mother. That's it. Now, make a bow, and say *Quack!*"

The little birds did as they were told. Meanwhile, all the other ducks in the yard were eyeing them up, and one of them said out loud, "Look at that rabble! As if there weren't enough of us already. And look how ugly that one is! We can't put up with him!" And the duck flew at the ugly duckling and pecked him in the neck.

"Leave him alone," said the mother. "He's not doing any harm."

"He is gawky and different, so he must be put in his place."

"Now, now," said the old duck with the red rag on her leg. "The other ducklings are all very pretty; it's just this one that doesn't seem to have hatched right."

"If you please, my lady," said the mother, "he may not be handsome, but he's good-natured, and swims just as well as the others – maybe better. I'm sure his looks will improve, and he won't stay so outsized; it's just that he stayed so long in the egg, that's all that's wrong." And she plumed his neck for him and smoothed out the feathers. "Besides, he's a drake, so looks aren't everything. He's fit and strong, so he'll be able to look after himself."

"Anyway, the others are charming," said the old duck. "Make yourselves at home, and if you happen on an eel's head, my dears, that would be very welcome."

So they made themselves at home.

But the poor little duckling who was last out of the egg and looked so ugly got jostled, and pecked, and teased by ducks and hens alike. "You big booby!" they all mocked. And the turkey, who was born with spurs and carried himself like an emperor, puffed up his feathers like a ship in full sail and ran straight at him, all red in the face and gobbling. The poor little thing was quite beside himself, what with being so ugly, and being the butt of every joke.

That was just the first day; after that, it got worse and worse. Everyone picked on the ugly duckling. The ducks bit him; the hens pecked him; the girl who came to feed the poultry kicked him out of the way. His own brothers and sisters looked down on him, and jeered "Yah! Boo! Hope the cat gets you!" One day, even his mother sighed, "If only you were far away."

So he ran away. He fluttered over the hedge, and frightened some little birds that flew into the air. "That's because I'm so ugly," he thought, and shut his eyes. But he kept on going, until he came to a wide marsh, where wild ducks lived. He lay there all night, worn out and miserable.

In the morning the wild ducks flew up to have a look at their new companion. "What in the world are you?" they asked, and the duckling squirmed this way and that, trying to be polite.

"You really are an ugly-mug," said the wild ducks. "But that doesn't bother us, as long as you don't want to marry into our family." Poor thing! He wasn't dreaming of getting married; all he wanted was to be allowed to sleep among the reeds, and drink a little marsh water.

There he lay for two days, and on the third two wild geese came along – or, rather, two young wild ganders, full of high spirits and self-importance. "Listen, kid," they said, "you may be a freak, but you make us laugh. Come with us and we'll show you a good time. There's another marsh nearby full of tender young geese, the sweetest creatures who ever said '*Hiss!*' A clown like you will really tickle their fancy."

"*Bang! Bang!*" a gun fired twice. Both the young ganders fell dead in the reeds, and the water was stained red with their blood. "*Bang!*" went another gun. Flocks of wild geese rose into the air. "*Bang! Bang!*" A big shoot was on. Hunters lay all around the marsh; some were even sitting in the trees at the edge. Clouds of blue gunsmoke curled over the water and drifted among the trees. The gun-dogs splashed through the mud, flattening the reeds. The poor little duckling was so frightened. He tried to bury his head beneath his wing, but just then a fierce dog bounded up to him, its tongue slobbering from its mouth and its eyes flashing fire. It opened its gaping jaws and lunged at the duckling, but then it was gone with a splash, without touching him.

The duckling sighed in relief. "I am so ugly, even the dogs don't want to sully their mouths with me." Then he lay quite still, listening as shot after shot rained down on the marsh.

It was late in the day before it grew quiet, and even then the poor duckling didn't dare to move for several hours. Then he hurried away from the marsh as fast as he could; he ran over fields and meadows, struggling against the strong wind which had got up.

Near nightfall he reached a wretched little cottage, so tumbledown that it couldn't decide which way to fall, which was the only reason it remained standing. The wind howled, and the poor duckling had to sit on his tail so as not to be blown over. It grew worse and worse. Then the duckling noticed that the cottage door had lost one of its hinges, and was hanging awry. There was just enough of a crack for him to creep inside; so he did.

An old woman lived there, with her cat and her hen. The old woman called the cat Sonny; he could arch his back and purr, and even send out sparks if you stroked him the wrong way. The hen had bandy little legs, and so was called Chickabiddy-Shortshanks; she was a very good layer, and the old woman loved her dearly.

Next morning, they all noticed their strange new guest. The cat purred, the hen clucked, and the old woman said, "Whatever's up?" Her sight was failing, and she thought the ugly duckling was a plump full-grown duck that had lost its way. "What a find!" she said. "Now we shall have duck's eggs; unless it's a drake. Time will tell."

And so the duckling was taken into the household, on three weeks' trial; but didn't lay any eggs.

Now the cat was master of the house, and the hen was mistress. They always talked about "We and the world," because they thought they made up half the world, and the better half at that. The duckling tried to put another opinion, but the hen wouldn't allow it.

"Can you lay eggs?" she asked.

"No."

"Well, then, hold your tongue."

And the cat asked, "Can you arch your back? Can you purr? Can you give out sparks!"

"No."

"Then keep your opinions to yourself, when your betters are talking."

So the duckling sat alone in the corner, feeling very low. He tried to think about the fresh air, and the sunshine, but that just made him long to go for a swim. At last, he couldn't help telling the hen about it

"That's just a sick fancy," said the hen, "It's because you're idle. You should lay an egg, or purr, then you'd forget all this nonsense."

"But it's so delicious to swim on the water," said the duckling. "It's wonderful to dabble about, and dive to the bottom."

"If that's what you call delicious," said the hen, "then you must be mad. Go and ask the cat – he's the one with the brains – if he wants to go swimming in all that wet water. Ask the old woman, our mistress, the wisest woman in the world! Do you imagine *she* wants to dabble and dive?"

"You just don't understand," said the duckling.

"Well, if we don't understand, who would? If you think yourself wiser than the cat, or the old woman, or even myself, you've got another think coming. So don't be silly, and count your blessings. Haven't you come to a nice warm room, with good companions who can teach you a thing or two? But you're too stupid for words, and I can't be bothered with you. Believe me, I wish you well, but I must speak as I find – it takes a real friend to point out home truths. So why not make a bit of effort in return: try to lay an egg, or purr, or give out sparks."

"I think I had better go back out into the wide world," said the duckling.

"Well, go then," said the hen.

So the duckling went. He swam on the water; he dived down – but he made no friends, and he thought that was because he was ugly.

Autumn came. The leaves in the wood turned yellow and brown; the wind caught them and whirled them into a dance; the sky grew steely; the clouds hung heavy with hail and snow; the raven perched on the fence squawked "*Caw! Caw!*" in the cold air. It was enough to give anyone the shivers, and the poor duckling had a hard time of it.

One evening, just as the setting sun flamed across the sky, a flock of large, lovely birds rose from the rushes. The duckling had never seen such beautiful birds; they were brilliant white, with long, graceful necks. They were swans. They called out – a harsh, compelling "Honk!" – spread their magnificent wings, and wheeled away, flying to the warm lands, where the water didn't freeze over.

They soared high, so high, and the ugly duckling was seized with a wild excitement. He turned round and round in the water like a millwheel, craning his neck to keep them in sight, and let out a cry so shrill and strange that he scared himself. Oh! he would never forget those noble birds. When they were lost to view, he plunged to the bottom of the water; when he rose again he was almost beside himself.

He did not know what the birds were called, he did not know where they were going, and yet he felt drawn to them in a way he had never felt before.

He didn't envy them – such beauty was utterly beyond him. Not even the ducks would put up with him – poor, ugly creature.

The winter was cold; bitter cold. The duckling had to swim round and round in the water to stop it from freezing over. Every night, the little circle of free water grew smaller; the duckling had to work his legs frantically to keep the ice at bay; at last, he was worn out, and the ice froze him fast.

Early next morning a peasant saw him, and broke the ice up with his wooden clog, and took the duckling home to his wife.

The duckling soon revived, and then the children wanted to play with him. But the duckling was afraid, and fluttered panic-stricken into the milk-pail. The milk splashed everywhere; the wife screamed and clapped her hands; the duckling flew into the butter-tub, then into the flour-bin, and out again. What a sight he was! The wife shouted, and tried to hit him with the fire-tongs; the children cackled and shrieked as they chased him about the room. It was just as well that the door was open; the duckling sprang through, and hid in the bushes on the new-fallen snow; he lay there in a daze.

It would be too sad to tell you all the hardships the duckling had to endure through that hard winter. He was huddling in the shelter of the reeds on the moor when one day the sun began to shine warmly again, and the larks sang: spring had arrived.

The duckling stretched out his wings. They were stronger than before, and carried him swiftly along. Almost before he knew it he was in a big garden with blossoming apple-trees, and sweet-smelling lilac overhanging a stream. It was so lovely; so fresh, and spring-like.

From the thicket ahead came three beautiful swans, ruffling their feathers and sailing calmly on the water. The duckling recognized the stately creatures, and was overcome with a sudden sadness.

"I will fly to them, those noble birds," he said. "They may peck me to death for daring to approach them, ugly as I am; but I don't care. Better to be killed by them than to be bitten by the ducks, pecked by the hens, kicked by the girl who feeds the poultry, and left to freeze in the winter."

He flew down and landed on the water, and swam toward the glorious swans. As they caught sight of him, they darted toward him, ruffling their feathers. "Kill me, if you will," said the poor creature, and he lowered his head to meet his death. But what did he see reflected in the water! He saw his own likeness – no longer a gawky, ugly duckling, but a swan!

It doesn't matter if you don't fit in in the farmyard, if you've been hatched from a swan's egg.

This was the end of all his suffering – this blissful happiness. The three great swans swam round him, stroking him with their beaks.

Some little children came running into the garden. They threw corn and bread into the water, and the littlest one called out, "Look, there's a new swan!" The others shouted with delight, "Yes, a new one!" They clapped their hands, and cavorted with pleasure, and ran to tell their father and mother. They threw bread and cake into the water, and everyone said, "The new one is the most beautiful of all – so young and handsome!" And the older swans bowed before him.

He felt quite overcome, and shyly tucked his head underneath his wing, he was so flustered. He was almost too happy; but not proud, for a good heart is never vain.

He thought of how he had been persecuted and despised, and how he heard everyone say that he was the most beautiful of all these beautiful birds. The lilacs bowed their branches to him on the water, and the sun sent down its welcoming warmth. His heart was filled with joy. He ruffled his feathers, and stretched his slender neck, and said, "I never dreamed of such happiness, when I was the ugly "duckling!"

THE GOLDEN GOOSE

There was once a man who had three sons. The youngest of them was
called Dimwit, and the others were always mocking him and never
missed a chance to put him down.

One day the eldest son went into the forest to cut wood. His mother gave
him a cake and a bottle of wine to keep him going.

When he reached the forest, he met a little old white-haired man, who said,
"Good day to you. I'm hungry and thirsty. Give me a piece of your cake and
a drink of your wine."

The clever son replied, "What I give to you, I take from myself. Be off
with you!"

He started to cut down a tree, but it wasn't long before he missed his
stroke and gashed open his arm, so that he had to go home and have it
bandaged. That was the little old man's doing.

Then the second son went into the forest with a cake and a bottle of wine
that his mother gave him. He too met the little old white-haired man, who
asked him to share his food and drink. But the second son replied cleverly,
"If I give it to you, I won't have it for myself. Be off with you!"

He shouldn't have crossed the little old man. After only a few strokes at the tree, he cut himself in the leg and had to give up.

Then Dimwit said, "Father, let me go and cut wood."

The father replied, "Your brothers, who are clever, have tried it, and they have both hurt themselves. You know nothing, so you should leave it alone." But Dimwit begged and pleaded, and at last his father said, "If you hurt yourself, you'll just have to learn the hard way." His mother gave him a cake made of water and ashes, and a bottle of sour beer.

When he got to the forest, he too met the little old white-haired man, who greeted him and said, "Give me a piece of your cake and a drink from your bottle. I'm so hungry and thirsty."

Dimwit replied, "I've only got an ash cake and some sour beer, but you're welcome to share it."

So they sat down to eat, and when Dimwit brought out the cake, it was rich and sweet, and when he uncorked the bottle, the sour beer had turned into fine wine. So they ate and drank, and then the little old man said, "Because you have a good and generous heart, I will give you good luck. If you cut down that tree over there, you will find something in the roots. But don't take it home to your mean-hearted brothers." And with that the little old man went away.

Dimwit cut the tree down, and in its roots he found a goose with feathers of pure gold. He picked it up in his arms, and carried it to a nearby inn, where he thought to stay the night. The innkeeper had three daughters, and when they saw the golden goose they were fascinated. They all wanted the golden feathers.

The eldest daughter thought, *I shall soon have a chance to pull out a feather*. When Dimwit went to bed, she grabbed hold of the bird's wing. As soon as she did so, her hand stuck fast.

The second daughter then came along with the same intention, but no sooner had she touched her sister's arm than she too was stuck like glue.

When the third daughter came, the two stuck sisters shouted, "Don't come near! Don't come near!" But she just thought they were trying to keep the golden goose for themselves, so she took no notice. As soon as she touched the second sister, she too was caught. So they had to spend the night stuck to the goose.

Next morning Dimwit picked up the goose in his arms and went on his way. He didn't trouble himself about the girls who were hanging on to it, and they had to keep up with him as best they could, running now left, now right, as the fancy took him.

When the parson saw them trotting this way and that across the fields, he called out, "For shame, you good-for-nothing girls! Running after a young man like that! Is that any way to behave?" And he caught hold of the youngest's hand. Then he too was stuck and had to run along with the others.

The sexton saw them running past, and called out, "Where are you going? Don't forget there is a christening today!" He ran after them, and caught the parson by the sleeve, and then he was stuck too.

They called out to two peasants they passed, "Help us!" But as soon as the peasants touched the sexton, they too were stuck. So now there were seven of them running along behind Dimwit and the goose.

Later that day they came to a city where there was a king whose daughter was so solemn that she never laughed. The king had decreed that the first man who could make her laugh should marry her. When Dimwit heard that, he ran in front of her with the golden goose under his arm, and the seven stragglers running along behind.

When the princess saw the procession, she couldn't help herself. She began to laugh, and once she had started she could scarcely stop. So Dimwit

said to the king, "Can I marry her now, then?"

The king was not very keen on Dimwit for a son-in-law, so he said, "Not quite yet. First, you must find a man who can drink my cellar dry."

Dimwit went back to the forest to look for the little old white-haired man. When he got to the place where he had felled the tree, he found a miserable-looking man sitting on the ground.

"What's wrong?" asked Dimwit.

"I'm so thirsty!" said the man. "I can't abide cold water, and though I've just drunk a barrel of wine, that was no more use than a raindrop on a bonfire."

"I can help you there," said Dimwit. "Just come with me, and you shall quench your thirst." He led him to the king's cellar, and the man set to work. He drank and drank until every barrel was dry, from the table wine to the rare vintages.

Dimwit went to the king, and said, "All the wine's gone. Can I marry her now?"

"Not quite yet," said the king. "First you must find a man who can eat all the bread in the palace bakery."

Dimwit went back to the forest, and in the place where he had felled the tree he found a man who was tightening a belt around his waist, with a look of terrible pain on his face. "What's wrong?" Dimwit asked.

"I'm so hungry!" the man replied. "Though I've eaten a whole ovenful of bread, that's like a crumb instead of a feast to a man with an appetite like mine. My stomach's empty."

"I can help you there," said Dimwit. "Come with me, and you shall eat your fill."

He took him to the palace bakery. The king had called in all the flour in the kingdom, and it had been baked into a huge bread mountain. But the man

from the forest just went up to it and started eating, and by the end of the day it was all gone.

"Now can I marry her?" said Dimwit to the king.

"There's one last thing," the king replied. "You must come and fetch her on a ship that sails both on land and on water."

Dimwit went back to the forest, and this time he found the little old white-haired man, who said, "When I was hungry and thirsty, you shared your food and drink with me. Now that you need my help, I will give it, because you were kind to me." And the little old man gave him a ship that could sail in the air over both land and water.

When the king saw Dimwit sailing through the air towards the palace, he knew that he would have to keep his word. So Dimwit and the princess were married and lived happily together, because he could always make her laugh. And after the king died, Dimwit inherited his kingdom.

SNOW WHITE

Once in midwinter, when the snowflakes were falling like feathers from the sky, a queen sat sewing at a window, and the frame of the window was wrought of black ebony. And as she was sewing, and gazing at the falling snow, she pricked her finger with the needle, and three drops of blood fell on the snow. The red looked so striking on the snow that she said, "I wish I had a child as white as snow and as red as blood and as black as this window frame."

A short while after that, she gave birth to a daughter. Her skin was as white as snow, her lips and cheeks were as red as blood and her hair was as black as ebony. They called her Snow White, and when she was born, the queen died.

A year later the king took a second wife. She was a beautiful woman, but proud and haughty, and she couldn't bear anyone else to be more beautiful than she was. She had a magic mirror, and when she looked in it she would say,

Mirror, mirror, on the wall,
Who is the fairest of them all?

and the mirror would answer,

You are the fairest of them all.

And then she would preen herself, because she knew the mirror spoke the truth.

But as Snow White grew, she became more and more beautiful. By the time she was seven years old she was as beautiful as the day and more beautiful than the queen. So one day when the queen said to her mirror,

Mirror, mirror, on the wall,
Who is the fairest of them all?

the mirror replied,

You are the fairest in this hall;
Snow White is the fairest of them all.

The queen turned yellow with shock and green with envy. From that moment, whenever she looked at Snow White, her heart turned over in her breast, she hated the girl so much.

Envy and pride began to strangle her heart, like weeds in a flower bed. She knew no peace, night or day. So at last she sent for a huntsman and told him, "Get that child out of my sight. Take her into the forest and kill her and bring me back her heart and her liver as proof."

The huntsman obeyed. He took the child into the forest, but when he had drawn his knife and was about to pierce Snow White's innocent heart, she began to weep, and said, "Ah, dear huntsman, let me live! I will run away into the wild forest and never come home again."

As she was so beautiful, the huntsman took pity on her and said, "Run away, then, you poor child." And though he thought to himself, *The wild beasts will eat her soon enough,* still he felt as if a stone had been rolled from his heart, as he no longer had to kill her. Just then a young boar came running by, and he stabbed it and cut out its heart and liver to take to the queen as proof that the child was dead. And the wicked queen ordered the cook to stew them with salt, and she ate them, thinking she was eating the heart and liver of poor Snow White.

Meanwhile Snow White was all alone in the forest. She didn't know what to do. She was even afraid of the leaves on the trees. She started to run over sharp stones and through spiky thorns, and the wild beasts ran past her and did her no harm.

She ran as far as her legs would carry her. Then, just as night fell, she came to a little cottage and went inside to rest. Inside, everything was small, but so neat and clean. There was a table with a white cloth, and on it were laid seven little plates, each with its own knife, fork, spoon and mug. Against the wall were seven little beds, all in a row, covered with white linen.

Snow White was very hungry and thirsty, but she did not want to eat all of anyone's meal. So she ate some from each plate, and drank some from each mug. Then, as she was so tired, she laid down on each of the beds in turn, until she found one that suited her, the seventh. Then she said a prayer and fell asleep.

When it was quite dark, the owners of the cottage came back.

They were seven dwarfs who mined the mountains for silver and gold. They lit their seven candles, and when they could see, each saw that something had been moved.

The first said, "Who's been sitting in my chair?"

The second said, "Who's been eating off my plate?"

The third said, "Who's been using my spoon?"

The fourth said, "Who's been using my fork?"

The fifth said, "Who's been using my knife?"

The sixth said, "Who's been drinking from my mug?"

And the seventh said, "Who's that sleeping in my bed?"

He called the others over, and they came running to see. The light from their candles fell on little Snow White as she lay there fast asleep, and they whispered, "What a lovely child!" and took care not to wake her. The seventh dwarf slept with the others, one hour with each in turn, and so the night passed.

In the morning, Snow White woke and was frightened when she saw the seven dwarfs. But they were friendly and asked her, "What is your name?"

"My name is Snow White," she said.

"And how do you come to be in our house?"

And she told them how her stepmother wanted to have her killed but the huntsman had spared her life, and how she had run all day through the forest until she came to their cottage.

The dwarfs said, "If you will take care of the house for us – do the cooking, make the beds, wash, sew and knit, and keep everything neat and clean – you can stay with us, and we will look after you."

"Oh yes," said Snow White. "I'd love to."

So she stayed and looked after the house while the dwarfs went off to dig and delve, and in the evening when they came home she had a warm supper ready for them. She was alone all day, so the kindly dwarfs warned her, "Beware of your stepmother. She may find out you are here, so don't let anyone in."

Believing that she had eaten Snow White's heart and liver, the queen was sure that she was once more the most beautiful of all. But when she asked her mirror,

> *Mirror, mirror, on the wall,*
> *Who is the fairest of them all?*

it replied,

> *You are the fairest in this hall;*
> *Snow White is the fairest of them all.*
> *Beyond the forest and over the hills,*
> *With the seven dwarfs she dwells.*

The queen was taken aback, but she knew that the mirror never lied. She realized that the huntsman must have deceived her and that Snow White must still be alive.

She thought and thought how she might kill her for until she was once again the fairest in the land, envy would eat her up. At last she made a plan. She dressed up as an old pedlar woman and made up her face so that you would never have known it was her.

She crossed the mountains in disguise and came to the house of the seven dwarfs. She knocked at the door, crying, "Pretty things for sale! Going cheap!"

Snow White looked out of the window, and called, "Hello, old woman. What have you got to sell?"

"Nice things, nice things," she answered. "Stay-laces woven of bright silk." And she pulled out one of the pretty laces.

Snow White thought, *This old woman has an honest face. I can let her in.* And she opened the door to her and bought a lace.

"Child," said the old woman, "you look a fright. Let me lace you properly."

Snow White stood and let her put in the new lace. But the old woman laced her so quickly and tightly that she couldn't breathe, and she fell down as if dead.

"Now I am the most beautiful," said the queen, and she hurried away.

Shortly the seven dwarfs came home. What a shock they had, to find Snow White lying on the floor! She wasn't breathing, and they thought she was dead.

They lifted her up and, seeing how tightly she was laced, cut the lace. She took in a little breath and, little by little, she came to life again. When the dwarfs heard what had happened, they said, "The old pedlar woman must have been the queen in disguise. You've got to be careful and not let anyone in when we are not here."

When the wicked woman got home, she stood in front of her mirror and asked,

Mirror, mirror, on the wall,
Who is the fairest of them all?

It replied,

> *You are the fairest in this hall;*
> *Snow White is the fairest of them all.*
> *Beyond the forest and over the hills,*
> *With the seven dwarfs she dwells.*

When she heard that, all her blood rushed to her heart with hatred. So Snow White was still alive! "Never mind," she said, "I'll think of something." She thought over all her worst spells, and then, muttering under her breath, she made a poisoned comb.

Then she disguised herself as another old woman. She made her way across the hills to the house of the seven dwarfs and knocked at the door, crying, "Pretty things for sale! Going cheap!"

Snow White looked out of the window, and called, "Go away! I can't let anyone in."

"But there's no harm in looking, is there?" said the old woman, and she held up the poisoned comb.

It was so pretty that Snow White thought, *This old woman seems harmless. I can let her in.*

She opened the door, and the old woman said, "Your hair is all tangled. Let me comb it for you." Snow White stood there patiently, and the old woman jabbed the poisoned comb into her hair. As soon as it touched her, Snow White fell down senseless. "Much good may your beauty do you now," said the wicked woman. "You are done for." And she went away.

It wasn't long before the dwarfs came home. When they saw Snow White lying as if dead, they at once suspected her stepmother. They checked her over, and found the poisoned comb. When they took it out, Snow White began to come to. She told them what had happened, and they warned her again to take care and not to open the door to anyone.

When the queen got home, she went straight to her mirror.

Mirror, mirror, on the wall,
Who is the fairest of them all?

It replied,

You are the fairest in this hall;
Snow White is the fairest of them all.
Beyond the forest and over the hills,
With the seven dwarfs she dwells.

When she heard the mirror speak, she trembled and shook with rage. "Snow White must die!" she shrieked. "Even if it costs me my life." Then she went to her secret room and made a poisonous apple. It was white with a red cheek, and looked so delicious that anyone would have been tempted; but whoever ate even the tiniest piece of it would die.

When the apple was ready, she made up her face and disguised herself as another old woman and made her way across the hills to the house of the seven dwarfs. She knocked at the door, and Snow White put her head out of the window straight away, and said, "I can't let anyone in. The seven dwarfs told me not to."

"It's all the same to me," said the old woman. "I'm just giving away apples. Here, have one."

"No," said Snow White. "I daren't."

"Are you afraid of poison?" said the old woman. "Look, I'll cut the apple in two. You have the red cheek, and I'll have the white." The apple was so cunningly made that only the red cheek was poisonous.

Snow White longed for the apple, it looked so perfect, and when she saw the old woman eating the white half she couldn't resist. She reached out and took the poisonous half. As soon as she bit into it, she fell down dead.

The queen gave her a cruel look, and cackled, "White as snow, red as blood, black as ebony! This time the dwarfs cannot wake you up."

This time when she asked her mirror,

> *Mirror, mirror, on the wall,*
> *Who is the fairest of them all?*

the mirror replied,

> *You are the fairest of them all.*

Then her envious heart was at peace – as much as a heart can ever be.

When the dwarfs came home that evening they found Snow White lying lifeless on the ground. They lifted her up, searched her for anything poisonous, unlaced her, combed her, washed her with water and wine, but this time they could not revive her.

The dear girl was dead, and dead she remained. They laid her on the table, and all seven of them sat around it and wept for three whole days.

Then they were going to bury her, but she still looked as if she were alive, with her beautiful red cheeks. They said, "We can't bury her in the dark ground." So they had a coffin made out of glass, so that she could be seen from all sides, and they laid her in it, and wrote her name on it in golden letters, and that she was a king's daughter. They they put the coffin on the top of the hill, and one of them always stayed by it to watch over it. And the birds came and wept for Snow White: first an owl, then a raven, then a dove.

Snow White lay there in her coffin for a long, long time. She didn't decay but lay as if she were asleep. She was still as white as snow, as red as blood, and as black as ebony.

One day, a prince came into the forest, and spent the night at the house of the seven dwarfs. He saw the coffin on the hilltop and the beautiful Snow White inside it, and he read what was written on it in golden letters. Then he said to the dwarfs, "Let me have the coffin. I will give you whatever you want for it."

"We wouldn't part with it for all the money in the world," they replied.

Then he said, "Then let me have it as a gift, for I can't live without being able to gaze on Snow White. I will love her forever."

Then the dwarfs took pity on him and gave him the coffin. The prince's servants picked up the coffin to carry it away on their shoulders. One of them tripped over a tree stump, and the jolt shook the poisoned apple from Snow White's throat, where it had lodged. So before long she opened her eyes, lifted the glass lid of the coffin, and sat up. She was alive again!

"Oh!" she cried. "Where am I?"

The prince was filled with joy. "You are with me," he said, "and I love you more than the whole world. Come with me to my father's palace and be my wife."

As soon as she saw him, Snow White loved him too. She went with him, and soon they held their wedding feast.

Snow White's wicked stepmother was invited. When she had put on all her finery, she stood in front of her mirror and asked,

> *Mirror, mirror, on the wall,*
> *Who is the fairest of them all?*

And the mirror replied,

> *You are the fairest in this hall;*
> *The bride is the fairest of them all.*

The wicked woman spat out a curse. She was so wretched she didn't know what to do. At first she didn't want to go to the wedding, but she couldn't help it. She just had to go and see the prince's bride.

As soon as she saw her, she recognized Snow White. She wanted to run, but she couldn't move for rage and fear. Iron slippers had been put into the fire. They were fetched out with tongs, and set before her. Her own envy and shame forced her feet into the red-hot shoes, and she danced in them until she dropped down dead.

THE PRINCESS AND THE PEA

There was once a prince who wanted to marry a princess – only she must be a real princess. He went all over the world looking for one, but there was always something wrong. He found plenty of princesses, but were they real princesses? He couldn't quite tell; there was always something that didn't feel right So he came back home, very put out, because he did so long for a real princess.

One evening there was a fearful storm. The rain came down in torrents, and the thunder and lightning were quite terrifying. In the middle of it all there was a knock at the palace gate, and the old king went to open it

Standing outside was a princess. Goodness! What a state she was in. She was drenched. The water was running through her hair and down her clothes, in at the tips of her shoes and out at the heels. Yet she said she was a real princess.

"We'll soon see about that!" thought the old queen. She didn't say a word, but went into the spare bedroom, stripped the bedclothes, and placed a pea on the base of the bed. Then she piled twenty mattresses on top of the pea, and twenty featherbeds on top of the mattresses. That was the princess's bed for the night.

In the morning they asked her how she'd slept

"Oh, shockingly," said the princess. "I hardly got a wink of sleep all night. Heaven knows what was in the bed; I was lying on something hard, and it has made me black and blue all over. It's quite dreadful."

So they could see that she was a real princess, as she had felt the pea through twenty mattresses and twenty featherbeds. Only a real princess could be as sensitive as that.

So the prince married her, now he knew for certain she was a real princess. And the pea was put in the museum, where you can see it for yourself, if it hasn't been stolen.

That's a real story!

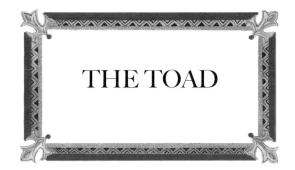

THE TOAD

The well was deep, so the bucket was on a long rope, and water was hard to fetch. Although the water was clear, the sun never reached down far enough to touch it; but as far as it did shine, green moss grew between the stones.

A family of toads lived there. They were newcomers; they had followed their mother when she fell head over heels down the well. The green frogs, who had lived there swimming in the water for ages, called them "cousins," and pretended the toads were only on a visit. But the toads had no intention of leaving. They liked it in the "dry part" of the well, as they called the damp stones.

Mother frog had once been on a journey - all the way to the top in the water bucket. But the light hurt her eyes. Luckily she managed to scramble out of the bucket and fall back *splash!* into the well where she lay for three whole days with a bad back. She hadn't much to tell about the world above – only that the well was not the whole world. Mother toad could have told them more than that, but she never answered when she was spoken to, and so they never asked her.

"She's fat, ugly and slimy," said the children, "and her brats are slimier still."

"That's as may be," said mother toad, "but one of them has a precious jewel in their head – or is that me?"

The young frogs didn't like the sound of that; they pulled faces at her and dived back into the water. But the young toads stretched their hind legs in sheer pride, and held their heads perfectly still.

Then they pestered their mother. "What is it we're being proud of?" they asked. "What is a jewel?"

"It is something so valuable and fine," said mother toad, "that I can't begin to describe it. You wear it for your own pleasure, and to upset other people. And that's enough of your questions; I've said my say."

"Well I'm sure I don't have the jewel," said the littlest toad. "It sounds too precious for the likes of me. And if it would upset other people, it wouldn't give me pleasure. All I wish is that I could go to the top of the well, just once, and look out. That must be wonderful."

"Best stay put," said mother toad. "You know where you are here, and here's where you belong. Stay out of the way of that bucket, or it might squash you; and if you do get caught in it, jump out. Though there's no guarantee you'll land as well as I did, with legs and eggs intact."

Croak! said the littlest toad, as if she were swallowing her words.

But she still longed to go to the top of the well and glimpse the green world above; so next morning when the water bucket was lowered, the little toad, quivering with excitement, jumped off its ledge into the full bucket, and was hauled to the top.

"*Ugh!* What an ugly brute!" said the man who had pulled it up – and he poured the water away and aimed a kick at the toad. She only just escaped being badly hurt by hopping into some nettles.

In among the nettles, the toad looked up and saw the sun shining through the leaves, which seemed transparent; it was the same as when we go into a tall wood and look up to the sun filtering through the high branches.

"It's much nicer here than in the well," said the little toad. "I could stay here forever." She stayed for one hour; she stayed for two. But then she began to wonder what lay beyond the nettle patch. "As I've come this far, I might as well go on."

She hopped out onto a road. The sun was hot on her back, and she was soon coated with dust from the highway. "This really *is* dry land," she said. "It's almost too much of a good thing; it's making me itch."

She came to the ditch, where forget-me-nots and meadowsweet grew; in the hedge were elder and hawthorn, twined round with flowering bindweed. What a picture it was! And there was a butterfly fluttering about, which the toad decided must be a flower that had left home to see the world – and that was quite a shrewd guess.

"If only I could go so fast," said the toad. *Croak! Croak!* "It's so nice here."

She stayed in the ditch for eight days and nights, and never went short of food. But on the ninth day she thought, *I must be getting along.* Though it was hard to imagine that anywhere could be more delightful than the ditch, yet it was lonely; and the wind last night had carried the sounds of other toads or frogs.

"It's wonderful to be alive," she said, as she set off once more. "It's wonderful to come up out of the well, to lie in a forest of nettles, to march across a dusty road and to rest in a wet ditch; but I must go on. I'll look for those other toads or frogs, for one can't do without company. Nature is not enough!"

She made her way through the hedge into a field and across it to a pond surrounded by reeds.

"Isn't this a bit wet for you?" said the frogs who lived there. "But you're welcome all the same – a girl just as much as a boy."

They invited the toad to join them for a singsong that evening. A lot of bellowing in squeaky voices   you know the kind of thing. There were no refreshments, just all the water you could drink.

"I must be getting on," said the little toad. She felt a desire for something better.

She saw the stars twinkling in the sky; she saw the new moon; she saw the sun rising ever higher. *I am still in a well*, she thought. *But a bigger well. I must go higher yet. I'm so restless; I feel strange longings in me.*

Later, when the moon was full, the poor creature thought, *I wonder if that is the bucket being lowered down for me to jump into. That would take me higher! Or maybe the sun is the great bucket – it shines so brightly, and I'm sure it's big enough to take us all. I must take my chance when it comes. Oh! how my head is filled with its light. I'm sure it gleams brighter than any jewel. So I don't regret not having one of those. I just want to go higher; higher to glory and joy. I have faith, and yet I'm fearful. The first step is so hard; but I must go on – onwards and upwards!*

And she put her best foot forward, and soon came back to the road. Then she came to a place where humans lived – there were both flower and vegetable gardens, and the toad rested under a cabbage leaf.

"How many different creatures there are!" she said. "There's always something new in this big, lovely world! As long as you keep on the move!" She took a look around the vegetable garden. "How green it is!"

"I should say it is," said a caterpillar that was sitting on a cabbage leaf. "And my leaf is the greenest of them all. It's so big it covers half the world; but that's the half I don't bother myself about."

Cluck! Cluck! The hens were coming. The one at the front had the sharpest eyesight – she spied the caterpillar on the leaf and pecked at it. It fell to the ground and lay there wriggling. The hen peered at it first with one eye and then with the other, wondering what all that wriggling was for. *It can't be doing it for fun*, she thought; and she lifted her head to strike.

The toad was horrified, and began to crawl at the hen.

It's called up reinforcements, thought the hen. *A horrible crawling thing! It would only have tickled my throat, anyway.* So she left the caterpillar alone.

"I wriggled out of that one," said the caterpillar. "I kept my nerve. But the problem is, how do I get back onto my cabbage leaf? Where is it?"

The little toad offered her sympathy to the caterpillar and said she was glad her ugliness had frightened the hen away.

"What do you mean?" said the caterpillar. "I saved myself by my own wriggling. Though it's true you are ugly. I don't owe you a thing. Now where's my leaf? I smell cabbage. . . . Here it is! There's no place like home. But I must climb up higher."

Yes, higher! thought the little toad. *Ever higher! It feels just as I do. A fright like that would give anyone a funny turn. But we all want to go higher.*

The little toad looked up as high as it could. On the farmhouse roof was a stork's nest, and father stork and mother stork were chatting away with their long beaks. *Imagine living so high up*, thought the toad. *If only I could go up there!*

Inside the farmhouse lived two students. One was a poet, and the other was a naturalist. The first sang and wrote about the wonder of God's creation, and how it was mirrored in his heart. His poems were short and simple yet full of meaning. The second looked at the world itself, in all its individual parts. He considered the creation as a matter of science – add here, take away there, and eventually the sum works out. He wanted to know and understand it all. He had a searching mind; a fine mind. They both loved life.

"Look, there's a good specimen of a toad," said the naturalist. "I'll catch it and preserve it in alcohol."

"You've already got two. Leave it in peace," said the poet.

"But it's so wonderfully ugly," said the naturalist.

"If only we could find the precious jewel in its head, it might be worth dissecting it," said the poet.

"Precious jewel!" said the other. "What kind of natural history is that?"

"It's folklore, not natural history. I like the thought that the toad, the ugliest of creatures, has a precious jewel hidden inside its head. It's the same way with human beings – think of the precious jewels that Aesop and Socrates had inside their ugly mugs."

The two friends walked away, and the toad escaped being preserved in alcohol. So she didn't hear any more and didn't understand half of what she had heard. But she knew they had been talking about the precious jewel. *It's just as well I don't have it, or I might have been in trouble*, she thought.

Father stork was still chattering away on the roof. He was giving his family a lecture, and keeping an eye on the young men in the garden at the same time. "Human beings are the most conceited of all animals," he said. "Listen to them jabbering away in their silly lingo. They're so proud of being able to speak, yet if they travel as far as we storks go in a single day, they find they can't understand a word! Whereas we storks speak the same tongue all over the world – the same in Egypt as in Denmark."

"And humans can't fly at all! They have to get in a machine that does it for them, and then they break their silly necks in it! It gives me shivers up and down my beak to think of it. The world can do without them. We don't need them; all we need are frogs and worms."

What a magnificent speech, thought the little toad. *The stork must be a very important creature, it lives so high up. I've never seen anything like it.* Just then the stork launched itself into the air. *And it can swim too!* thought the toad.

Meanwhile mother stork was telling her children all about Egypt, and the waters of the river Nile, and all the glorious mud to be found in foreign parts. It all sounded wonderful to the toad.

"I must go to Egypt," she said. "If only the stork will take me with him –

or perhaps one of the youngsters would. I'd pay him back somehow. Yes, I'll go to Egypt, I'm sure of it. I'm so lucky. I'm sure my dreams are better than any precious jewel."

But she *did* have the most precious jewel – her endless longing to go upwards, ever upwards. That was the jewel, and it gleamed with joy and yearning.

At that moment the stork came. He had seen the toad in the grass. He snatched her up in his beak, squeezing her in half. It hurt, but the little toad was sure she was going to Egypt. Her eyes shone with anticipation – it was as though a spark was flying out of them.

Croak!

Her heart gave up; the toad was dead.

But what of the spark that flew from her eyes? What of that?

The spark was caught up in a sunbeam and carried away. But where was it taken, that precious jewel from inside the toad's ugly head?

Don't ask the naturalist; ask the poet. He'll tell you the answer in a fairy tale. A caterpillar will be in the story; and a family of storks, too. The caterpillar transforms itself into a butterfly; the stork flies right across the ocean to Africa, then finds the shortest way home again to Denmark – back to the very same nest. It's almost too magical and mysterious – yet it's true. Go and ask the naturalist – he'll have to admit it. And you know it yourself, for you have seen it with your own eyes.

But what about the jewel in the toad's head? Seek it in the sun! You might find it there!

But the light is too bright. We do not have eyes that can gaze on all the glory that God has created. But we shall get them one day. That will be the most wonderful fairy tale of all; for we shall be in it ourselves.

THE WATER
OF LIFE

There was once a king who was so sick, everyone thought he was going to die. His three sons were very sad. They sat in the palace garden and wept. There they met an old man who asked them what the trouble was. They told him their father was very ill and would surely die. The old man said, "I know of a cure, and that is the water of life. If he drinks some of that, he will get well again. But it is hard to find."

The eldest son said, "I will find it." He went to the sick king and asked leave to go and search for the water of life. "No," said the king, even though it might cure him. "It's too dangerous." But the son begged and pleaded until the king gave his consent. For the prince thought in his heart, *If I bring him the water of life, my father will love me best, and I shall inherit the kingdom.*

So he set out, and on his journey he met a dwarf, who asked him, "Where are you going so fast?"

"What's it to you, you little runt?" said the proud prince.

So the dwarf cast a spell on him, so that he rode into a narrow ravine and got stuck. He could not move forwards or backwards, but was confined as tightly as if he were in prison.

The sick king waited and waited for him to return. When he did not, the second son begged leave to go and look for the water of life. He too thought, *If I find the water, then the kingdom will fall to me.*

The second son also met the dwarf, and dealt with him just as high-handedly. So the dwarf cast a spell on him, so that he too rode into a ravine and could not escape. That's the fate of haughty people.

When the second son did not return, the youngest begged to be allowed to go and seek the water of life. He thought, *I can save my father and my brothers too.*

When the dwarf asked him, "Where are you going so fast?" he told him, "My father is dying, and I am seeking the water of life, to cure him."

"Do you know where to look?" asked the dwarf.

"No," admitted the prince.

"As you have spoken kindly, and not haughtily like your brothers, I will help you. Soon you will reach a castle. In its courtyard is a fountain, and from that fountain springs the water of life. But it is an enchanted castle, and you will not be able to enter without this iron wand and two loaves of bread, which I will give you. You must strike the castle's iron door three times with the iron wand, and it will open. Inside are two lions with gaping jaws. You must throw each of them a loaf, and they will be quieted. Then hurry and collect some of the water of life before the clock strikes twelve, or you will be shut in again and never get out."

The prince thanked him for this advice, took the wand and the bread, and went on his way. When he reached the castle, everything was as the dwarf said. The door sprang open at the third stroke of the wand, and when he had quieted the lions with the bread, he made his way into the castle.

He came to a large, splendid hall full of enchanted princes. He took the rings from their fingers, and also a sword and a loaf of bread that he found there. Beyond the hall was a room in which he found a beautiful girl. She was overjoyed to see him. She kissed him and told him that he had set her free. "My kingdom will be yours," she said. "Return in a year, and we shall be married. But hurry now, and collect the water of life before it strikes twelve."

He went on through the castle, and came to a bedchamber with a beautiful newly made bed in it. He was very tired, so he lay down for a little rest. He fell fast asleep, and when he awoke, the clock was striking a quarter to twelve. He jumped up in a fright, ran to the spring, drew some water in a cup that he found there, and hurried away. As he was escaping through the iron door of the castle, the clock struck twelve, and the door came crashing down so fast it cut off a piece of his heel.

He was delighted to have found the water of life, and set off for home. On the way he met the dwarf. When the dwarf saw the sword and the loaf he said, "Those are great treasures. With the sword you can slay whole armies, and the loaf will never be finished, no matter how much you eat."

But the prince was only interested in finding his brothers. "What has happened to them?" he asked. "They set out in search of the water of life before I did, but they have not returned."

"They're stuck in ravines," said the dwarf. "I sent them there because they were so proud and overbearing."

The prince begged the dwarf to release them, and he agreed.

But he warned, "Do not trust them. They have wicked hearts."

When his brothers joined him, he was glad to see them all the same. He told them all about his adventures, and how he had found the water of life,

and brought a cupful away with him, and how he had freed a beautiful princess from enchantment, and how she was waiting for him and in a year they were to be wed, and he was to have her kingdom for his own.

On their way they passed through three kingdoms in which war and famine were raging. In each of them, the young prince lent the king of the country his sword, in order to defeat his enemies, and the loaf, in order to feed the people. Then they got on a boat and sailed for home.

The two older princes got together on the voyage and said, "Our brother has found the water of life, not us. For that our father will give him the kingdom. It should be ours by rights. He is nothing but a thief." And so they plotted to destroy him. They waited until he was asleep, and then they stole the water of life from the cup and replaced it with salt seawater.

As soon as they arrived home, the young prince took the cup to the king, expecting him to drink it and be cured. But as it was seawater, it made him worse than ever. As he was retching, the two older princes came to him and told them they feared their brother had tried to poison him. Then they gave him the true water of life.

As soon as the king drank the water, he was cured.

After that, the king made much of his two older sons but distrusted the younger. The older princes even bragged to their brother how they had deceived him, but there was nothing he could do about it, for his father would not have believed a word of it.

Thinking that the young prince had tried to murder him, the king decided he must die. He ordered his huntsman to shoot the prince when they were riding in the forest. But the man could not bring himself to do it and warned the prince to stay away from court.

The king was happy to think that his son was dead. But then three wagons of gold and jewels arrived, all for his youngest son. They were presents from the grateful kings of the three kingdoms that he had saved from war and famine. Then the king wondered, *What if I was wrong? What if he was innocent after all?* And he spoke aloud, "I wish he were still alive and that I had not ordered him killed!"

The huntsman heard these words and confessed to the king that he had not carried out the order but had let the prince go. At that a weight fell from the king's heart. He had it proclaimed in every country that his son was free to come home again.

Meanwhile the princess had ordered a golden road to be built leading to her castle, and told her guards, "The man who rides right up the middle of this road is the man for me. Anyone who rides alongside it is a liar, and you are not to let him in." When the year was nearly over, the eldest son thought he would seek out the princess and pretend to be her rescuer. When he came to the gleaming golden road, he thought, *It would be a shame to mark this road by riding over it,* so he rode his horse along the verge. When he came to the iron door of the castle, the servants would not let him in.

Then the second prince set out, but he too thought it would be a shame to ride over the magnificent golden road, and rode along the verge. So the servants would not let him in either.

When the year was quite over, the youngest son remembered the princess who was waiting for him and set off to find her.

When he came to the golden road, he saw it shining right up to the castle gate, and said to himself, *This will lead me to my love.* He rode his horse right up the middle of the road to the castle gates, and the servants let him in.

The princess welcomed him with joy, and they were married straightaway. She told him that he was now lord of all her kingdom. "But first, you must go to your father, who has forgiven you, and tell him all that has happened." So he rode home, and told the king how his brothers had betrayed him. The

old king wanted to punish them, but they had fled to sea in a ship, and they never came back as long as they lived.

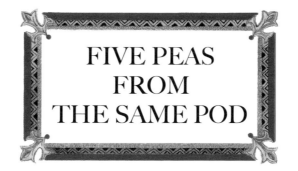

FIVE PEAS
FROM
THE SAME POD

There were once five peas in a pod; they were green, and the pod was green, so they thought that the whole world was green, and that was quite right. The pod grew and the peas grew; they all made space for each other, five in a row. The sun shone and kept the pod warm, and the rain fell and kept it clean. It was a snug little home, light in the day and dark at night, just as it should be. As the peas grew, they began to think for themselves; after all, they had to do something to pass the time.

"Shall I be stuck here forever?" each said in turn. "I'm afraid I'll get hard from sitting here so long. I wonder if there's something outside; I have a feeling there is."

Weeks passed. The peas turned yellow and the pod turned yellow. "The whole world is turning yellow," they said, and they had a perfect right to say it.

Then they felt the pod being pulled; they were in a man's hand, being shoved into a pocket alongside some other pods. "Soon we shall be opened," they said. That's what they were waiting for.

"I wonder which of us will go farthest," said the smallest pea. "We'll soon see."

"What will be, will be," said the biggest.

Pop! The pod split, and all five peas rolled out into the bright sun. They were in a little boy's hand. He said they were just the peas for his peashooter.

He fired off the first.

"Now I'm flying out into the wide world! Catch me if you can!" and it was gone.

"I shall fly right up to the sun," said the second. "That's the pod for me!" And off it went.

"We don't care, so long as we keep rolling!" said the next two, for they were rolling on the floor. But they went into the peashooter anyway. "We'll go farthest!" they cried.

"What will be, will be," said the last pea, as it was shot into the air. It lodged in a crack in the attic windowsill; the rotten wood was already stuffed with moss and earth, and the pea stuck there. It lay hidden, though not hidden from God.

"What will be, will be," it said.

In the little attic room lived a poor woman who did heavy work, such as cleaning stoves and chopping wood. But though she was strong and willing, however hard she worked she was still as poor as ever. Living with her was her daughter, who had been lying in bed for a whole year. The little girl was terribly thin and delicate; it seemed she could neither live nor die.

"She'll go to her little sister," said the woman. "I had two children, but it was so hard to look after them both, so God went shares with me and took one for himself. I'd like to keep the other, but God doesn't want them to be parted, so she'll go to her sister."

But the sick girl stayed on. She lay patient and quiet in bed all day, while her mother went out to earn their keep.

It was spring, and one sunny morning, just as the mother was getting ready to go out to work, the girl noticed something through the lowest

windowpane. "Whatever is that green thing, peeping in at the window? It's swaying in the breeze."

The mother opened the window a crack. "Well!" she said. "It's a little pea plant; you can tell by the green leaves. However did that get there? It will be a little garden for you to look at."

So the sickbed was moved nearer to the window, so the girl could keep an eye on the pea as it sprouted, while the mother was at work.

"I feel I'm getting better, Mother," said the young girl that evening. "The sun has been shining in on me so warmly today. The little pea is getting stronger, and so am I. Soon I will be out in the sunshine, too!"

"I hope so," said the mother, but she did not believe it. Still, because the little plant had given her daughter such cheer, she found a stick and tied it up, so that the wind wouldn't break it. And she ran a string up the window, to give the pea something to climb up, which it did. You could see it grow from one day to the next.

"I do believe it's going to flower," said the mother one morning, and now she too began to hope that her sick daughter might get well. She thought how lately the girl's talk had been livelier, and how each morning she sat herself up in bed and looked with sparkling eyes at her little garden of one pea plant.

Next week, the girl got up for the first time and sat happily in the sunshine for a whole hour. The window was open, and the pea's pink flower was in bloom. The girl leaned out and kissed the delicate petals. That was a red letter day.

"God himself planted that pea and made it thrive to bring hope to you and joy to me, my darling," said the happy mother, and she smiled at the flower as though it were an angel from heaven.

But what happened to the other peas? The one who flew out into the wide world shouting, "Catch me if you can!" was swallowed by a pigeon. He lay in its stomach like Jonah in the whale. The two who didn't care did no better, for they were eaten by pigeons, too, so at least they made themselves useful. But the other one – the one who wanted to fly up into the sun – that one fell down into the gutter and lay there for weeks in the dirty water. It began to bloat.

"I'm on the way up," it said. "Soon I shall be so fat I shall burst, and that's as much as any other pea can do, or has ever done. I'm the most remarkable of the five peas in our pod."

And the gutter agreed.

But the little girl stood at the attic window with shining eyes and glowing cheeks. She folded her delicate hands over the pea flower and gave thanks to God for it.

"I still think my pea's the best," said the gutter.

THE
GOLD
CHILDREN

There were once a poor man and woman who had nothing but a little hut. They fished for their living and lived from hand to mouth.

One day the man cast his net and caught a fish that was all of gold. As the man gaped down at his catch, the fish said, "Throw me back into the water, and I will change your hut into a castle."

"What use is a castle if I have nothing to eat?" the fisherman replied.

The gold fish told him, "In the castle there will be a cupboard which, whenever you open it, will be full of wonderful food."

"In that case," said the fisherman, "we have a deal."

"There is just one condition," said the fish. "If you tell anyone where your good luck has come from, you will lose everything."

The man threw the gold fish back into the water. When he got home, his hut was transformed into a magnificent castle, and his wife was dressed like a queen. "Husband," she said. "Look what's happened! I like it!"

"Me too," he said.

"But we still don't have anything to eat."

"Don't worry about that,' said the husband, and he opened the cupboard that was indeed full of wonderful food.

"What more could the heart desire?" said the wife. "But where has it all come from?"

"Don't ask me that," he replied. "If I tell you, we'll lose it all."

"Well, if you don't want to tell me, that's all right," she said. But she didn't mean it. She couldn't rest until she knew. She pestered the poor man day and night until he told her about the gold fish. But as soon as the secret was out of his mouth, the castle disappeared, and they were back in their old hut again.

The husband had to go back to fishing for a living. But as luck would have it, he caught the gold fish again. He made the same deal as last time, and when he got home the castle was back. But once again his wife nagged him until he told her what had happened, and once again they lost everything.

The man went fishing once again, and for a third time he caught the gold fish.

"I can see that it is my fate to fall into your hands," said the fish. "Take me home and cut me in six pieces. Give your wife two of them to eat, give two to your horse, and bury two in the garden, and they will bring a blessing."

The fisherman did as he was told. From the two pieces he buried in the ground sprang two golden lilies; the horse had two golden foals; and his wife gave birth to two boys with bodies of gold.

The boys grew tall and handsome, and the lilies and the horses grew with them. One day the boys said, "Father, we want to ride out into the world on our golden horses."

He was sad, and said, "But how will I bear it? I won't know how you are."

They answered, "As long as the golden lilies stand tall, all is well with us. But if they droop and fade, we shall be ill. If they wither, we shall be dead."

They rode off and came to an inn full of people who laughed and jeered at the gold children. Hearing their mockery, one of the boys was so ashamed that he didn't want to go on; he turned his horse around and rode home to his father and mother. But the other boy carried on.

He reached the edge of a great forest. The people there warned him, "Don't go into the forest. It's full of robbers. When they see that you and your horse are made of gold, they will kill you."

But he would not be frightened off. He took bearskins, such as tramps wore in those days, and covered himself and his horse with them, so that the gold could not be seen. He set off into the forest. Before long he heard voices. One said, "Here comes someone." The other replied, "It's only a tramp. Let him go; he looks as poor as a churchmouse." So the gold child rode through the forest and nothing harmed him.

One day he came to a village, where he saw a girl so beautiful that he thought there could not be anyone more beautiful on earth. His love was so strong that he went up to her and said, "I love you with all my heart. Will you marry me?"

She liked the look of him just as much, and she answered, "Yes, I will be your wife and be true to you my whole life long."

Just as the priest was making them man and wife, her father came home. He was very suprised to find his daughter getting married. "Who's the bridegroom?" he asked, and the gold child was pointed out, still wrapped in his bearskins.

The father said angrily, "No tramp is going to marry my daughter!" He wanted to kill him.

But the bride begged for his life, saying, "He is my husband, and I love him with all my heart." And in the end her father calmed down.

Still, he wasn't happy. The next morning he got up early to take a look at the man and see if he really was just a common tramp. When he looked into the room, he saw a magnificent golden man lying sprawled across the bed.

The cast-off bearskins were tumbled on the floor. *What a lucky escape!* he thought. *In my anger I might have committed a terrible crime.*

That night the gold child dreamed that he was hunting a splendid stag, and when he woke he told his wife, "I must go hunting."

She was worried and begged him to stay, saying, "I'm afraid something bad will happen to you." But he would not be dissuaded.

He went into the forest, and it wasn't long before a fine stag appeared just as in his dream. He aimed, and was about to shoot, but the stag ran away. He chased it all day, over hedges and ditches, without ever catching it. In the evening, he lost its track.

There was a cottage nearby. It was a witch's house. The gold child knocked at the door, and the witch answered. "What are you doing in the forest so late in the day?"

"Have you seen a stag?"

"Oh yes, I know the stag well," she said.

Then a little dog came out of the cottage and started barking ferociously at the gold child.

"Be quiet, you beast, or I'll shoot you," he said.

"What?" cried the witch in a temper. "Would you kill my dog?" She turned him to stone, and he toppled to the ground.

His bride waited in vain for him to come home. She thought, *The bad thing I dreaded has come to pass.*

Back at home, the other gold brother was standing beside the gold lilies when one of them suddenly drooped. "Something terrible has happened to my brother!" he said. "I must go to his aid."

The father begged him to stay at home. "What if I lose you too?"

But he said, "I must go, and I will."

He mounted his gold horse and rode into the forest where his brother was

lying, turned to stone. The old witch came out of her cottage and called to him. She wanted to turn him to stone too. But he was too clever for her. He did not go near her, but shouted, "Bring my brother back to life, or I will shoot you."

The witch didn't want to, but she touched the stone with her finger, and it came back to life.

The two gold children hugged each other and kissed. They were full of joy. Then they rode out of the forest, one home to his bride, the other to their father. The father said, "I knew the moment you saved your brother, for the gold lily suddenly stood up as fresh and straight as ever."

They all lived happily their whole lives long.

THE
FLYING TRUNK

O nce there was a merchant who was so rich that he could have paved
the whole street with silver. But he didn't actually do that because
he had other ideas about what to do with his money. Before he spent
a copper coin, he made sure he would get a silver one back. That's the sort of
merchant he was. A merchant he lived, and a merchant he died.

All his money now went to his son, who had a high old time with it. He
went dancing every night, made paper kites out of folding money and
skimmed gold pieces over the lake instead of stones. That's the way the
money goes, and it did. Soon he had nothing left but four pennies, a pair of
slippers, and an old dressing gown. His friends wouldn't have anything more
to do with him; they didn't want to be seen with him on the street. But one of
them, in a friendly spirit, sent him an old trunk, with the advice, "Get
packing!"

A fat lot of good that was – he didn't have anything to pack. So he packed
himself.

It was a strange trunk. As soon as you pressed the lock, it took off into the
air. And that's what it did now! Up it flew, with the young man in it, up the
chimney, through the clouds, and off into the wild blue yonder.

The bottom of the trunk kept creaking, and the young man was scared it would fall to bits – and then, heaven help me, he'd have had to learn some fancy acrobatics fast. But at last he landed in Turkey.

He hid the trunk in the woods and walked into town. He felt right at home, as the Turks all went around just like him in dressing gowns and slippers. Then he met a nurse with a baby. "Nurse," he said, "what is that big palace over there, with the high windows?"

"That is where the princess lives," she replied. "It has been foretold that she will be unlucky in love, so no one is allowed to visit her unless the king and queen are there."

"Thank you," said the merchant's son, and he went back to the wood, got into his trunk, flew up to the palace roof, and crept in at the princess's window.

She was lying on her sofa asleep. She was so lovely that the merchant's son couldn't stop himself from kissing her. This woke her up, and she was scared out of her wits until he told her he was a god, who had come down to her from the sky. That cheered her up.

They sat side by side on the sofa, and he told her stories about her eyes. They were like dark deep lakes, he said, in which her thoughts swam like lovely mermaids. He told her about her forehead – it was like a snowy mountain, with wonderful caves full of treasure. And he told her about the stork, which brings dear little babies. Oh, he said wonderful things. So when he asked her to marry him, she said yes.

"Come back on Saturday," she said, "and have tea with the king and queen. They will be so proud when I tell them that I am going to marry a god. They love stories, so you must be sure to have a good one to tell them. My mother likes high-class stories with a proper moral, and my father likes funny ones that makes him laugh."

"I shall bring a story as my wedding gift," he said. Before they parted, the princess gave him a sword decorated with gold coins – those would come in useful!

So he flew off and bought himself a new dressing gown, and then he settled down in the woods to make up a fairy tale for the king and queen. It had to be finished by Saturday, and that's not as easy as it seems.

But at last the story was done, and Saturday had come.

The king and the queen and the whole court were at the princess's for tea; and the merchant's son was most gracefully received.

"Now you must tell us a story," said the queen. "One that is both profound and instructive."

"And funny," said the king.

"I'll try," said the merchant's son.

This is the story he told. Listen to it carefully.

Once upon a time there was a bundle of matches, who were very proud because they came of such noble stock. Their family tree – of which each of them was but a chip – had been a huge old fir tree in the forest. So now, as they lay on a shelf between a tinderbox and an old iron pot, they reminisced about their glory days.

"Yes," they said, "those were the days. We were at the very top of the tree! Diamond-tea – that is to say, dew – every morning and evening, nonstop sunshine from dawn to dusk, when the sun was shining, and all the little birds eager to tell us their stories. We were so rich we could afford to wear our best green clothes all year round; other trees spent the winter in rags and tatters. But at last the revolution came – that is to say, the woodcutter – and we were laid low. The family was split up. The trunk got a job as a mainmast on a schooner that can sail right round the world if it wants to; the branches

had business here and there; and we were entrusted with the task of spreading light among the common people – that's what gentlefolk like us are doing down here in the kitchen."

"It's not been like that for me," said the iron pot which was next to the matches on the shelf. "From the moment I came into the world I've been scrubbed and put on to boil – I've lost count of the times! My job's the foundation of the home – so I'm the most important one in it. My only respite is to sit on the shelf after I've been scoured clean and enjoy a little after-dinner conversation with my friends. But apart from the bucket, which does get out to the well every so often, we're all real stay-at-homes. Of course the shopping basket does bring us all the gossip, but she's a regular firebrand, always jabbering on about the government and the people. Why, the other day her wild talk gave one old jug an apoplectic fit, and he fell down and broke into pieces."

"You do rattle on," said the tinderbox. "Can't we just enjoy ourselves?" And he struck his steel against his flints so that the sparks flew.

"Yes," said the matches. "Let's discuss which of us is the most distinguished."

"No, I don't like to talk about myself," said an earthenware bowl. "Let's tell each other stories. I will begin with a story of everyday life; something we can all relate to."

And the bowl began, "On the shores of the Baltic, where the Danish beech trees grow . . ."

"What a beautiful beginning!" exclaimed the plates. "We're going to enjoy this!"

"There I spent my youth," continued the bowl, "in a quiet household where the furniture was always polished, the floors always scrubbed, and we had clean curtains every fortnight."

"How interestingly you put it," said the feather duster. *"Your story has a woman's touch, there's something so pure and refined about it."*

"I feel that too!" said the water bucket, and she gave a little jump of pleasure, so that some of her water splashed onto the floor.

Then the earthenware bowl carried on with her story – and the middle and the end were just as exciting as the beginning.

The plates all rattled with joy, and the feather duster took some parsley and crowned the bowl with a garland. She knew that would make the others jealous, but she thought, If I crown her today, she'll crown me tomorrow.

"I feel like dancing," said the fire tongs – and what a dance! When she kicked one leg up high, the old chair cushion split his seams. *"Don't I get a crown;"* wheedled the tongs; and she did.

Vulgar riff-raff, *thought the matches.*

Then someone called for a song from the tea urn; but the urn said it had caught a cold and could only sing if it was brought to the boil. But it was just giving itself airs; it never would sing unless it was at the table with the master and mistress.

Over on the windowsill was an old quill pen that the maid used. There was nothing remarkable about her except that she'd been dipped too far into the inkwell, which made her rather stuck-up. *"If the tea urn doesn't want to sing, she needn't,"* said the the pen. *"There's a nightingale in a cage outside; it can sing. Of course its voice is untrained, but we won't hold that against it this evening."*

"I don't think it's right," said the tea kettle, which was a singer itself, and half sister to the urn, *"for us to listen to a foreign bird. Is it patriotic? I think the shopping basket should decide.*

"This makes me sick," said the shopping basket. *"Sick to my stomach. What goings on! Isn't it about time we reformed the whole house and*

established a new order? That really would be something! I'll take full responsibility."

"That's it, let's have a riot!" *they all shouted – but just at that moment the door opened. It was the maid. They all stood still; no one made a sound. But there wasn't one of them who wasn't thinking,* I really am superior to the others; if it had been left to me, this evening would have gone with a swing.

Then the maid took the matches and lit the fire with them. My goodness, how they sputtered and blazed! *Now everyone can see that we are the best,* they thought. How bright we are! How brilliant!

And then they burned out.

"That was lovely!" said the queen. "I really felt I was right there in the kitchen with the matches. You must certainly marry our daughter."

"Absolutely," said the king. "Let's fix the wedding for Monday."

Already they regarded the young man as one of the family.

On the evening before the wedding, the whole town was illuminated. Cakes and buns were distributed to the crowd; and all the little boys shouted "Hurrah!" and whistled through their fingers. It was great.

I suppose I'd better do my bit, thought the merchant's son. So he bought some rockets and whizzbangs and every sort of firework he could lay his hands on, and flew up into the air with them.

Whoosh! They went off with a bang! Such a glorious spectacle had never been seen before. The crowd nearly jumped out of their skins, and they did jump out of their slippers. Now they were sure it really was a god who was going to marry the princess.

As soon as the trunk came to earth, the merchant's son left it in the woods and returned to town to hear what people were saying about his performance – and that was only natural.

Everybody was talking about it. They all had their own views, and they were all fired up about it.

"I saw the god himself," said one. "He had eyes like sparkling stars, and a beard like a foaming torrent."

"He wrapped himself in a cloak of fire," said another, "with cherubs nestling in the folds."

What wonderful things he heard – and the next day would be his wedding day.

Now he went back to the woods to climb back into his trunk – but where was it? A spark from the fireworks had set it on fire, and the trunk was burned to ash. So the merchant's son could never fly again, and he had no way of getting to the princess.

She waited for him on the roof all day, and she is waiting still. As for him, he goes around the world telling stories – but they are not so light-hearted as the one he told about the matches.

HANS THE HEDGEHOG

There was once a farmer who had plenty of money and land, but he was unhappy, because he had no children. Once when he went to town, the other farmers mocked him, so when he got home he said in a temper, "I must have a child, even if it's only a hedgehog."

So when his wife had a son, he was half human, half hedgehog.

His little legs were all right, but he was a hedgehog from the waist up. The mother was frightened. She couldn't even nurse him, because he was so spiky. She said, "Look what trouble your temper has got us into now."

But the farmer said, "There's no use crying over spilt milk. What shall we call the boy?"

And the wife said, "There's only one name for him: Hans the Hedgehog."

"Where shall he sleep?"

"We can't put him in a proper bed, because of his quills." So they strewed some handfuls of straw behind the stove, and that was his bed for the next eight years.

By that time his father was sick of him, and only wished he would die. But he didn't die, he just lay there behind the stove.

One day the farmer went to the fair and asked his wife what she would like

him to buy her. "A joint of meat and some white bread rolls," she said. Then he asked the servant, and she said, "A pair of slippers and some fancy stockings." And finally he asked Hans the Hedgehog, and Hans answered, "Bring me some bagpipes, if you please."

When he returned from the fair he gave his wife the meat and the rolls, and the servant the slippers and the stockings. Lastly he went to the stove and gave the bagpipes to Hans the Hedgehog. Then Hans said, "Father, please go to the forge and have the rooster shod. Then I'll ride away and never come back."

The father thought the loss of his rooster well worth it to get rid of Hans the Hedgehog, so he took it to the forge to be shod. When it was done, Hans mounted the rooster and rode away, with his bagpipes under his arm. But he took all the farmer's pigs with him, which the farmer hadn't bargained on.

Hans the Hedgehog went to live in the forest and tend his herd of pigs, which soon grew very large. The rooster sat on a branch of a tall tree, with Hans on its back, and Hans practiced his bagpipes until the music he got out of them was really beautiful. All this time, his father and mother had no idea what he was doing.

One day, the king got lost in the forest and heard the music. He sent a servant to find out what it was, and when the man returned he said, "Your Majesty, it is a hedgehog mounted on a rooster perched up a tall tree, playing the bagpipes."

The king was very curious and went to see Hans for himself and ask if he knew the way to the palace. So Hans came down from the tree and said, "I will show you the way if you will give me the first living creature you meet when we reach the palace courtyard."

The king took pen and paper and wrote something down and gave the paper to Hans, saying, "There, you have my written word on it." But he had written that Hans should not have the first thing he saw, for he thought, *He's only a dumb hedgehog, and I can write what I like.*

When he reached the palace, the first living creature the king saw was his daughter, running out to greet him. He told her what a joke it was that he had promised to give the first living creature he saw to the strange hedgehog who rode a rooster and played the bagpipes. "But don't worry," he said, "the promise isn't worth the paper it's not written on."

"That's just as well," said the princess, "for I wouldn't have gone with him, anyway."

Meanwhile Hans the Hedgehog lived happily in the forest, tending his pigs and playing his bagpipes.

It happened that another king got lost in the forest and made the same bargain with Hans in order to be shown the way home. But this king was an honest man. When his only daughter came running to greet him, he told her, "I was lost in the forest, and in order to find the way home, I promised to give the first living creature I met when I got back to a strange creature, half man and half hedgehog, who was sitting on a rooster in a tall tree, playing the bagpipes. I'm sorry, my dear, but that first living creature is you."

The brave girl said, "Never mind, Father. A promise is a promise, and I will go with him willingly if he comes to claim me."

After a while, Hans the Hedgehog had so many pigs that there wasn't room for them all in the forest, so he decided to go home. He sent word to his father that he was coming, with enough pigs for everyone in the village to have one. But his father wasn't pleased to see him, for he had hoped that Hans the Hedgehog had died years ago. So Hans said, "Father, take the rooster back to the forge and have him shod again, and I will ride away and never come back as long as I live." So his father took the rooster to be shod, and Hans rode away on him.

Hans rode to the kingdom of the first king. The king had given orders that if ever anyone came mounted on a rooster and playing the bagpipes, the army must kill him. So as soon as Hans appeared he was attacked from all sides. But he spurred on the rooster, and it rose into the air, right over the palace gates, to the king's window, and landed on the window ledge.

"Give me what you promised," said Hans the Hedgehog, "or I'll kill you and your daughter too."

The king was so frightened, he begged his daughter to save them by going out to Hans the Hedgehog. So she dressed herself in white, and her father gave her a carriage with six horses, and servants and a rich dowry. She got into the carriage, and Hans the Hedgehog got in beside her with his rooster and his bagpipes, and they drove away. The king thought he would never see his daughter again; but at least his own skin was safe.

They hadn't gone far when Hans the Hedgehog asked the princess, "Will you love me truly?"

"Yes," she said. But when he tried to kiss her, she turned away. His spikes caught her across the face, and left a smear of blood.

"You are false at heart," said Hans the Hedgehog. "Go home to your father, I don't want you." And no one else ever wanted her either.

Then Hans the Hedgehog rode on to the kingdom of the second king. This king had given orders that if anyone came riding a rooster and playing the bagpipes, he should be saluted, and brought to the palace at once.

When the king's daughter saw him she was frightened, for he did look very strange. But she told herself that it was wrong to judge people on appearances, and that anyway, a promise was a promise. So she welcomed Hans the Hedgehog with open arms, and they were married.

After the wedding feast, they went up to their room. She was still frightened, but Hans said, "Don't be afraid. I would never hurt you." Then he said to the king, "Tell four men to watch outside the bedroom door. When I go to bed I shall tear off my hedgehog's skin and cast it to the floor. They must rush in and throw it onto the fire, and watch until it is utterly devoured by the flames. Then I shall be free from the enchantment of my birth."

The men did as they were told, and when the skin was quite burnt up, Hans lay in the bed in human form, as shapely and handsome as could be. The king's daughter loved him truly, and the king named him his heir.

My tale it is done,
Away it has run
From my house to your house
To sit in the sun.

BELIEVE IT OR NOT

L isten, and you might learn something!
I saw two roast chickens flying along, their breasts to heaven and their backs to hell. I did.

I saw an anvil and a millstone swimming across the Rhine; they took their time about it, too. Ask the frog, if you don't believe me. He was sitting on the ice, quietly munching a cartwheel.

I saw a deaf man, a blind man, a dumb man and a lame man catch a hare. The deaf man heard it coming, the blind man spotted it, the dumb man shouted, "There he goes!" and the lame man ran and caught it by the collar.

Over their heads, I saw three men in a sailing boat, its sails billowing in the wind. Up, up they went, but at last they rose too high, and were drowned.

I saw a crab catch a mouse, and a cow climb a house. In that country, the goats are as big as flies . . . .

Phew! Open the window, and let out the lies.